STAR TAKER

VJ WAKS

ISBN: 978-0-988-3058-6-1

i

What can an eternity of Damnation matter to someone who has felt – if only for an instant – the infinity of Delight?
CHARLES BAUDELAIRE

STAR TAKER

PROLOGUE

For a long moment, the young man stood in the alcove doorway, staring back – at the bed.

The frame was heavy, oak, deeply carved, the covers tossed and tangled in the aftermath of passion's labours. The sleeper there stirred then reached across to the wand, which lay like a knife on the counterpane….

> *Mage, Sorcerer – Apprentice.*
> *Do not fear the Dark.*
> *Thou art the Dark.*
> *What dost Thou desire?*

Caspian Hythe jolted awake, with cold sweat on his brow and his breath coming hard and fast.

No. No. That was what I saw before – in the dream – the same dream that she had.

He rose from his bed. At the window, he thrust wide the casement, drawing the cool air of an early autumn deep into him.

This was not his room, not the room he had come to know as a youngster, to view as both sanctuary and prison as he grew older – left, and lost.

Both Mom and Dad.

And now, here I am in my father's room.

Moonlight cast a soft glow across the space.

He looked about him, seeing his father everywhere, and nowhere. The signature of a now-beloved man pressed close around him – and he was reminded it was not always so. For the young man who stood here now, a great deal had come to pass.

The loss – my rage – my anger at being left behind – my guilt. So here I stand in retribution of Randolph Hythe, a man I have only recently come to understand – to fathom – for one does not ever understand a mystery, one merely fathoms the depths.

It is a land unknown that I leave.

It is a land unknown I seek, to traverse, a journey of exploration – what he was, what he did, what he left me.

It is only just begun.

He crossed the room.

A sudden turn in the dark sent a stack of old books onto the floor. For a second, his footing was lost and Caspian Hythe – man – Mage – Sorcerer – found himself naked, on his hands and knees – staring in horror at what lay before him.

Ancient it was, hoary with age – with evil – for the guardians of its care and the boundaries of its control had been long dissolved. Open it lay; the dark leather of the cover lay rich but corrupt – with time, with content, and with the track of the sea's long, bitter wrath across the heavy surface.

Heavy – with evil; laden – for the Maker now slept – and the spells and the sentinels that had been forged and laid onto this terrible thing were gone, leaving it bare and eager to the unbridled lusts of men.

And its golden lock shattered – and the Mage watched spellbound as the golden chains shuddered before his eyes, shuddered and splintered, and cold mist rose from the surface of the Bane of Man – the Book of Books. Leering, page after page turned; pages led into pages, all inscribed and rife with sin, tenebrous with the shadows of darkness and light, age after age – abundant with villainy and age-old death.

And those pages called to him, in voices dark and fell, commanding him to *come*, to take up the Mastery, to release All within from their last, weakening bondage …

The man who was no longer just a man, whose face carried the weight of his past and terrible present, stumbled up.

He stumbled to the sideboard where the mirror rose in cold glory – and there before him was not his face, not the face of a young man, a young warrior – a young Knave – but the face of a woman, blazingly beautiful, with pale features and brilliant black eyes.

And the Mage hungered for Her, for Her power, Her magic, Her desire – with every part of his being, as Her ruby lips parted in a smile of longing and desire, with a welcome that would damn any soul to Hell.

He reached for that face as flame erupted from the frigid, smoking glass – and he was consumed, torn by the teeth of an immortal hunger – for life, for power – for ultimate dominion …

With a cry of terror, Caspian Hythe pulled back, away – now jolted completely awake.

Wild-eyed, gasping for breath, he was indeed in his father's bedroom, in his bed – one bathed in moonlight – where across the floor beside the bed, melting away like cursed snow – black, fetid, reeking with threat and corruption – the footprints of a woman's naked feet vanished before his eyes.

I am ready now.

CHAPTER 1

DANCE WITH ME

Thunder sounded distantly in a warning contretemps to the ageless, wordless dialog of steel on steel.

A moment later, Cass' blade was on the floor, spinning in a mad, razor sharp circle.

"Pick it up. What the Hell is the matter with you?"

Percy Onslow glared at Caspian Hythe.

The younger man's parry had been a travesty of poor aim and worse execution. Uncharacteristically speechless, Cass knelt to the sword. Sweat streamed down his face; his dark hair was matted, and the Mage's eyes were that dark grey blue that presaged strife – or worse.

Percy could not imagine what was in his opponent's mind. But this had been a stupid error, costly to life had it been any other and not himself at the other end of the blade.

With failure on his face, Cass rose with the sword and stared at the blade as if it were a stranger, rather than an easy and familiar extension of his arm, of his will, as it had always been in the past. Onslow stared as well.

Still unknown, at least to me, this man – this Sorcerer.

For this is the sword he used in the real past – the sword with runes of power, of warning – wrought into the living steel.

Through the line of the father – across the land '*Under*' – across centuries, surmounting the savage threat of the Black Queen's kingdom '*Below*' – the journey of this remarkable blade still amazed the sword master who now stood before that Sorcerer. In the comfort of his studio, where contention submitted to contemplation, where warfare rose to the level of art, where life and death was a poem, confined stanza by stanza within the limits of stance and steel, the teacher faced the student and again wondered exactly how little he could indeed teach him.

"Hold."

Percy went to him; with his gloved hand, he seized the bare blade and held it motionless – until Cass relaxed and released it to him.

The Mage turned away and paced angrily to the worktable where towels and water lay ready. Cass mopped face and shoulders; this was a Mensur bout and the two wore no protection other than their gloves. It had not been the first such trial. The scar across Percy's cheek, the line on Cass' arm bore witness to the severity – the earnest purpose of their training.

"Mr. Hythe."

The Mage's eyes stayed averted and wandering; there was no response.

"Caspian Hythe."

Cass looked up just in time, for Percy had tossed the blade back at him.

"Again."

Percy retreated; Cass looked at the sword and then at the teacher – advanced – and attacked. This time, sparks danced an angry jig off the edge of Onslow's blade.

Percy never saw the stroke coming.

One moment it was steel on steel, as before. The next saw the sword master's blade flung aside in a ferocious assault, a glittering sweep of whetted sharp silver that cut the air. The force of each blow was severe; for a second Percy thought his arm would break.

It was only the beginning. Cass would not relent and the teacher was suddenly at the mercy of the student.

Outside, the storm mirrored the drama within.

This time, lightening raked the sky as inside the studio, Percy Onslow, helpless, fell back from an onslaught so murderous, so unwavering that he could scarcely catch breath. And the eyes of Caspian Hythe – apprentice, Mage, Sorcerer – blazed with a terrible unholy light. Fire shone in Cass' eyes; it was a flame of darkness, beyond anger or ambition or the need to win.

Those eyes were inhuman; what Percy saw instead were the eyes of a demon, one roused to such wrath, such malevolence that death could be the only outcome.

"Cass!"

The cry went unheard; Cass did not stop.

Percy lunged sideways to escape the Mage's fury – it made little difference to the one less and less recognisable with each passing second. In the next moment the master lost his footing – Onslow slid heavily across the floor, the Sorcerer followed and Percy's hand came up, his voice rang in the studio, as rain thundered down outside and the room seemed to grow suddenly shadowed, almost too dark to see …

"Hold!"

As though turned to stone, the Mage froze.

But his blade was poised, its point aimed at Percy's heart – Cass' eyes were wide and wild, he stood drenched and nearly mad – then that terrible gaze went to the wide banks of windows as thunder tolled deafeningly. The building shook as lightning clove in two the tree at the end of the lane. The tree crashed down as thunder sounded again. With that sound the young man was there in body only – for Cass stood in spirit in a place so far away that the one on the floor could see no way to reach him.

4

He is there again, in that place – that time – nowhere near here.

What happened on that last day – in the past – to bring this horrific look into those eyes?

"Cass."

A long dreadful moment passed.

"Cass – look at me."

The Mage tore his gaze from the dark skies – agonised, he glared down on the man at his feet.

He stumbled back to the table – and flung the sword down on its surface.

"Keep it."

Slowly, Percy Onslow pulled himself to his feet and came to his side.

The interlude of terror had passed; now, only pity shone from Percy's eyes and his voice was as gentle as the hand he laid on his former pupil's arm.

"Go home."

That shouldn't have happened.

Inadequate; pitifully so, for an event that had so nearly cost a life.

He had not followed Percy's advice.

Instead, much less than half an hour later had found Cass on the Mount.

Cool and still, the cemetery beckoned with each pathway, each hillock crowned with grey stones. The storm had bypassed the tombs; bracing across his face was the fog that had begun to swirl about the

5

grey headstones marching in gloomy scatter across Guildford's oldest and most famed resting place.

Tendrils of clinging silver curled about his feet. The grey green stones leaned, wreathed in gossamer white, like the tattered shrouds of another age. His swift ascent of the hill had been Homeric; he had stopped at the ancestral Hythe home only long enough to leave his pack inside the door – that, and the sword with which he had so nearly killed Percy Onslow.

The look on Percy's face still stung.

Shock, wonder, and fear – fear of him.

Again.

An attack by a madman – an uncontrolled, vicious assault.

The exercise between pupil and the averred master had begun no differently than any half dozen training sessions since Caspian Hythe had returned from a fantastic, unimaginable past, to find his present restored – and to grieve.

Dad … and Fitzalan; I lost both. Abby was right.

I won; I succeeded, but success in that little visit into the past drew blood on both sides of time. What did I win?

I gave the future back to my friends, my family.

I lost Iain Fitzalan – and once more, Randolph Hythe.

I lost my father – again.

This time, the name that did not crowd his mind, rising like a welt of blood was that of Ava

Fitzalan. But the memory of the face and voice of the Knight consumed him, in heart and spirit since his return, since that awful moment before a ruined altar in a hidden grove where, in despite of power and need, defiant to any plea, to any command – a Gate would not open to him.

Time had passed – and not just in this time thread.

In misery, in anger and shame, now Caspian Hythe stood again where it had all begun. Where, just short months ago, he had come up, in bitterness, and had stood over the resting place of a genius whose own dreams had been darker than any had realised. Whose own voyage *'Below'* had rendered into stark, terrible life a world from nothing – who had given life to forces unnatural, to an Evil that the creator himself had never intended.

Lewis Carroll – who might have guessed how from the richness of his mind, such iniquity could spring?

He fell, trapped by forces he himself had enticed.

First summoned then ensnared, I followed him 'Below' into a universe of terror and wonder.

I had not gone there alone.

The cross that surmounted the last resting place of Lewis Carroll stood white and pure. Then mist swallowed it; Cass turned away. The fog sank, deepening into a white blanket about the headstones. As the Mage walked away, like muffled heartbeats were the sounds of his footfalls on leaves and turf until, without warning, as he had done so months before – he stood, frozen in shock.

Impossible; it can't be.

Yet, it was; real, terrifying – the ringing cry of an animal in pain – an animal somewhere on the Mount.

I will not go – not this time.

What is it to me; just another death.

Another death; surely, something had killed again. The whining dissonance fell away. Far more bizarre was the dreadful incongruity – for hope flooded the Mage's heart – it was the hope that the Gryphon had returned.

Deadly, still mysterious; yet, I do not fear him now.

So now, eagerly Cass followed, drawn by the sound of rustling in the densest vegetation that edged the graveyard's furthest rim. Here the fog was thinner, torn by the faint breeze on the hill and Cass ran past the monuments and stones.

At last, when the trail seemed as cold as the air; Cass looked up.

He stood at the loneliest limit of the grounds.

Over him, with weather-pitted face the hoary chiseled features of an angel gazed sternly down on the Mage. The icy marble gaze of the archangel Michael locked with that of the young man. A vagrant ray of sun pierced the clouds; light played along the edge of the blade held by the Prince of Heaven's legions, eerily illuminating the sword in the Protector's indomitable hand.

The Mage looked down; as if fallen from the carven figure's weapon, droplets of blood lay spattered over the grass.

They led him past the tombs to a thicket. As before, as in the discovery of the mangled fox months ago, he found the body of what had once been a stout badger. Still warm and supple, the torn, robust limbs steamed in the cold air.

The head was missing.

In eagerness to discover the track of the long talons, widely splayed – the singular spoor of the creature that did not exist – Cass knelt shivering on the frigid grass.

There …

He stared; he cursed.

There were indeed marks in the earth – but the pugs were enormous and wide, their edges vivid with blood. The marks of huge talons, hardened and grisly in strength lay before him. Deeply those talons had penetrated, sullying the hallowed earth.

And there, perched upright in dreadful parody – a dark message, a curt, choice expletive from Hell – the badger's head, with its mournful eyes clouded, its maw agape in agony, and those eyes stared back at the Mage.

This is not Gryphon's work.

He had no weapon; he needed one.

Wary, alert to every sound, any movement, Cass leapt to his feet.

Heart pounding, he stood waiting – listening.

Shadows were deepening; there could be no doubt as to the identity of the perpetrator – he knew what had killed here – what he had found was no more nor less than a gauntlet thrown down – bloody, riotously morbid, compelling.

And it came into his head – the *command*, insistent and resonant.

Find Quist – find Quist – find him now.

The message faded; the sender and the means stayed unknown.

Caspian Hythe did not wait to wonder.

He took to his heels – and ran.

CHAPTER 2

A WORD FOR A KNAVE

I am getting too old for this.

Montgomery Quist hauled himself up from the plank. The wood was cold; the protest in the Professor's seven decade old knees was profound this time. Like the calls of the crows scudding overhead, strident pain clamoured up and down his legs.

Rain was coming; it was time to leave anyway. The equivocation would get him no style points from the rest of his excavation team. He was the last; the others had had the sense to break off before the imminent threat from above. But he was, after all, still the head of that team.

Doesn't mean you have to go down with the ship, old man.

He looked up at the remains of the ruined church – the very same that had figured so prominently in such recent events.

Here it was, as Cass has said.

Here, in the nave of this now cursed place – a portal sleeps. It is still within. It waits.

A shiver crept over him.

The idea of something like a Gate—to anywhere, any when – took some getting used to.

The boy is still the only one who can work it, you fool – for all the rest of us – it sleeps.

As harmless as any loaded gun.

He retired his brushes to his kit.

Sweeping the dirt from trousers and hands, he eyed the clouds streaming in; it had gone curiously dark and chill, even for a day perilously close to true autumn. He managed to cover the gaping trench with the tarp, then secured its fluttering edges with the same heavy stones he'd removed to expose this new layer in this ancient site.

It was an old layer, indeed.

Millennia had passed since this well concealed sliver of history had seen day. Pots and bowls abounded; nearly untouched were the fragile trophies of a forgotten era. Here they had rested, secure from the ungentle hands of time. It was all Roman, or much earlier: ceremonial jugs, tools, daggers with their edges remarkably clean and sharp. And there lay a cache of splendid torcs, bronze bracelets, even a lunula, a curious molded cape fit for the shoulders of a small man, designed for one whose throat was long dust.

Bronze age gold, at the very latest.
And that ring – older by far, a masterpiece.
And it is not a lock ring, this was made for the hand – most strange.

The ring fascinated him; despite the danger of fingerprints and exposure after eons underground,

Quist still held it now in his bare hand. It was mesmerising; fine gold it was, delicately struck and worked with a small brilliant jewel set in its centre.

As if in harsh admonishment, the wind sprang into new life, lifting the Professor's white hair. He stood before the wreck of a doorway. It was the same ravaged spot where just weeks before, an infinitely strange young man had stood. The significance of the destruction of this place – what had transpired to bring that roof down – all of it struck him.

First fearful – then compelled – Caspian Hythe had been both. But Cass had gone; time had turned first back then forward in two separate journeys. He had worked a strange magic, a terrible one; that he had.

And he himself not unchanged by all that had transpired.

I thank the gods, dear fellow, for you – for what you did – and did not do.

Yet in my heart, I feel it is not yet finished.

For a work such as this, such a deed – it is the provocation of a veritable Prometheus.

That attracts attention at some level.

No, it is not quite finished I very much fear.

Reply came in the form of a sharp, angry roll of thunder. Lightning streaked across the distant hills. Quist's eyes went from the skies to those hills, far to the south and west. The storm was coming in, west of the Downs. That way lay Devon and the towns of the southern coasts, riddled with caves, rich with their tales of piracy and hidden treasure.

Ah well; it won't last.

He followed the fading echo of the sound and wondered from whence the next heaven's call might come. He regarded the weed choked drive. Then, just as he was about to return to his car, an unaccustomed look came across his face.

It had grown curiously dark around the church and a spate of cold drops flicked suddenly across his cheek.

Quist scooped up his kit.

He turned away from the car, and instead entered the frail sanctuary offered by the battered structure.

Even in the absence of half a roof, the space near the nave kept dry. Antiquity permeated the place. About him rose the odour of turned but still dank earth, of ancient stone and hopeful moss. Bright flashes of distant lightning etched windows long bereft of glass. It was a dismal place; the stone that remained was savaged – and not just by time.

Shadows mustered close around him.

For no more than the twentieth time, Quist picked his way toward the nave, whose intact beams had weathered much more than a great many winter's chill caprices. Traversing the singed and ragged hole that gaped above his head, and the bits of wood and masonry that somehow clung to the present, the black wings of two, then three ravens cut the heavy air.

Now he stood directly before the spot.

Indomitable, inviolate despite its age, a focus of both challenge and accrimination, there the altar stood.

Here it began – and ended – and continues?
Here is the altar where She worked such devilry.

Quist was long past the point of questioning anything Abigail Hythe's nephew might say, about this place and about a great many things. He had sat with them all, as, with truly astonishing reserve Cass had given a story beyond belief – of valor, of myth come to life, of fabled monsters and impossible deeds.

Beyond belief – no more.

That no one came here – either staff or stranger – he'd seen to it. This area had been long cordoned off, barred for good reason. Stoic and centred, with an old gold ring still in his hand, Montgomery Quist, Professor of Archaeology and student of all things arcane walked toward a stone altar, one whose sides were cracked but whose fundaments still endured – a relic that still plumbed the depths of ancient mystery.

A thing of the past – of all pasts?

Soundlessly, and independent of the weather outside, the air in the nave shifted.

Cass had warned him; he certainly should have known better.

Yet from the instant he had lifted up the ring, from the moment he had chosen to enter here, to approach the altar – a wheel had turned. The thunder had pealed its warrant, a soft, irresistible call had come from the far hills – and another voice had responded.

Compelled by words that rose inside his mind, commands that presided over and around his own thoughts, he stepped forward. Miles from where he stood, in a darkened room, words unbreathed in the clear air for countless years took form as invocation. And just as he had heard and obeyed in a dead man's rooms just weeks before, with his mind full of visions unforeseen and inexplicable, Quist obeyed now.

I stand here in this unhallowed place.

Yet, there it is, the scent of the sea. Out of shadow comes light – and how could I have missed it? Blue is not just a colour.

And there – what do I see?

Pages so ancient they should be crumbling, not turning in air that sings, and cries and calls – in a voice low and horrible.

What is it I am seeing?

What is it I am being made to see?

Dark was the nave.

Yet almost indiscernible, the faintest wisps of sapphire had began to pool about the cold, grey feet of the altar. Its cracked lid was still ajar, precisely as it had been on the day the Mage had stood beside it, studying the contents of a sepulcher, the bitter missives of cracked bone, of sinew hardened with age, of cloth shredded and stained with ancient blood. Bidden as in dream, Montgomery Quist advanced toward a Gate that had ceased a cold, watchful slumber – and had shifted stealthily into sentience.

For alive and ungovernable – light now glowed from the stones below the altar.

Quist still approached – and now his hand reached – a golden ring in his grasp, a ring whose metal gleamed with an unearthly fire, whose small circle seethed with glittering light.

"I wouldn't do that, you know."

The words were low, the voice at once silky and grating, in parody of human speech.

But it was enough; the fragile cords of the spell severed, and like a man startled awake from dream, freed from the grip of vision, Quist turned. With eyes wide and breath stertorous in the still of the terrible nave – he wheeled about.

Loud as a shout in a tomb, thunder came hard on the heels of his awakening. Quist stared back at the ruined doorway, the stone framework suddenly horrifically brilliant as lightning made bright the world of safety just beyond the door. His voice caught in his throat.

"Who?"

There came no answer; but the man of science gasped and cried out.

For eyes, brilliant, enormous and impossibly golden shone out of the darkness, a darkness cast not by cloud, or relic or the torrent of healthy rain – but the essence of darkness, one corrupt, hungry and infinitely evil. It was a shade that had suddenly blossomed into obscene life, a void and desecration cloaked in shadow, awful in substance.

Like gold come alive, pulsing with dreadful animation, with cursed liveliness – golden eyes fixed upon the man in the nave. With one hand over his suddenly aching chest, that man went slowly to his knees on the icy stones, as unnatural and impenetrable, darkness held sway all about him.

"Oh, you needn't bow," the voice chuckled. "It's not to *me* that you should kneel – *that* One is yet to come before you."

Quist's mind raced; a single word escaped his bloodless lips.

"Cat."

A purr, monstrous and resonant with infernal pleasure echoed from every corner of the edifice. Whatever was there in the dark now circled the man who trembled on the cruel floor. Tumbled masonry cut into his knees – as his senses faltered, threatening to quit the man entirely – his hand tightened upon the ring.

There came a deafening hiss from the Thing in the dark, a growl of hatred, of impotence – of undying vengeance.

A wave of vertigo swept through Quist.

His jaw set with sudden, unexpected force and resolve. His own speech seemed foreign to him, stronger by far than any he might have achieved even had he not been nearly prone and facing an imminent, bloody end – and had he but looked down upon it, within the jewel of the ring in his hand extraordinary changes were occurring …

"You may not touch this – not this, nor any here."

Those words had a chilling, unforeseen impact on the beast from Hell.

Bright with animosity, with hunger, the eyes of the Cat positively blazed.

Now the Thing came out of the shadow and Professor Quist saw the monster that Cass had fought and had vanquished *'Below'*. How the beast had conquered death Quist could not imagine; all he knew was that the killer's head was enormous, its massive shoulders were more than a meter from the floor – and that the foul light that glittered now in those golden orbs was remorseless, yet bitter with a fury stymied, a rage that had little power.

Somehow, I am inaccessible to that Thing; It cannot actually reach me.

Low but infinitely poisonous, the Cat's voice rang out.

"*Fool*. You invoke a power you cannot understand let alone control. *It is no friend to man – it will not save you – not you – nor him, in whose strength your trust is baseless.* For you shall bleed, and fall – and all your hopes shall perish with you. There will be time enough for you – old man. Time enough for my pleasure – and for His. Who will save you then? *No one.* As for now – I go to seek the Lady. Tell her – tell her – *we come*."

The taunt hung in air nightmarishly cold – Quist caught a glimpse of the huge body, with its striped and spotted fur – then he heard the hissing laughter fade away. He felt rather than knew he was now alone – and that the creature's malevolence was directed elsewhere.

Overcome by horror and a suffocating certainty of the Thing's next target, yet helpless to intercede – Montgomery Quist finally released his fragile hold on consciousness, and slid senseless onto the rank stones.

.

CHAPTER 3

SUM HIC

As mist from the Mount curled down into the garden, Abigail Hythe stood at the open door of the library.

An odd sense of presentiment had met her as she had come down that morning. It had been frightfully early. Even so, Cass had already left for a daybreak start with Percy Onslow. Since the day Cass had returned from the Castle ruins with its own, hidden toppled altar stone, her nephew had been increasingly reticent.

Increasingly agitated.

The Mage's days had been consumed by training, with a current of unsaid speeches – with portent. Although bound by her suspicions, Abby had not pressed a single issue. For, not one but every one of the events of the last few months had been like flags.

From the unusual change in season – to the tale in the Cards; all clarion.

Like banners, like calls – to arms.

Once again we are on the verge; we have seen a Knight and a Knave descend into the dark, into the heart of an unimaginable realm – we have seen one alone return. That one then rose in courage, in resolve and took up a terrible task.

Always, Caspian Hythe has taken up the challenge, always has he undertaken the thing at hand – always at great cost.

So does he continue to transform; for what are all the events of our lives if not milestones along a single path of transformation?

And my life is no exception.

New allies had rallied. Under Percy's harsh, pitilessly exact tutelage, the young man had found new discipline and prodigious focus. The sword master was a man as fierce, as tenacious as any Abby knew; her nephew had not yet seen the depth of Onslow's fidelity.

And buttressed with his vast knowledge and maturity, Quist is watching carefully, with resources that none of us expected.

Many had been the afternoon that the young man and the scholar had been closeted – in study, in exploration of the past.

What and where – these are now the questions.

For Quist had shown her the little map he had found in the library of Iain Fitzalan.

It had been no accident.

Iain's library was monumental, filled to overflowing with folios and ancient volumes – yet a small slip of parchment with a map had one day found its way into the Professor's hand. It had not been so much a find, as a gift. Even one as rigidly academic and skeptical as Monty had admitted to his astonishment that day – there had been a presence beside him in an otherwise vacant room, a presence not that of the owner of that home.

Now – presentiment – stronger every day since Cass' return from the past.

Abby had wasted no time. Delving into her books, deeply meditating – training – for dread had swiftly grown from vague unrest and its voice was now ever-present.

Be ready – beware.

She found time, and the need to lay her Tarot cards repeatedly. Repeatedly had they answered, and their results only fed disquiet.

Pages – Wands.

The Page of Wands – and now something else.

Something dire loomed, for she had not yet told her nephew of the events of just yesterday.

A visit to Monty's study for tea; it had started simply enough. Always enraptured by the relics and books of her friend even as Cass had been, the visitor had enjoyed her meal, surrounded by the trove of an eminent Archaeologist scattered in the room.

The need for an historian became suddenly paramount. For after tea, Quist had once again asked her to look over his find. It was, after all, just a map. It was when his guest asked him to draw the drapes and lower the lights – and she had lit the closest candle …

Strange how things sleep – in the earth, in water – or in a parchment – just waiting for the moment, the call – to awaken.

That day, something had awakened.

With the light sequestered, with the surge of candlelight sending a soft halo over Quist's desk – the parchment in Abby's hand had trembled, and turning abruptly, and all of its own accord – had floated down onto the desk. Now the reverse side was exposed directly to the candle light, and the Professor had watched, in silence and wonder as the lips of his old friend Abigail had moved in wordless whisper. And on the blank surface of the old paper, something came to life.

Much later, he would describe the words, with their long spidery tracings, as they had line by line come up from nowhere to march across the pale surface. Words sprang up where words had not been before and the two sat rapt on them.

In the Star Taker's realm,
Through the cave, past the Bone.
See the lad with the knife,
Who is seeking the Throne.
How he runs, see his eyes,
Blazing bright with his need.
See him near to the prize,
All intent on his deed.
Will he challenge the One,

Who guards Loch, Fen and Air?
Will he follow the Sun,
To the One who waits there?
All is found; all is made,
And the secret is clear:
When the Rose and the Maid
And the Master – appear.

A moment passed; letter by letter, the words faded and vanished and the parchment was blank and smooth once more. Long had the two friends sat in a room heavy with awe – with dread. Abby blew out the candle; Monty cast a dark eye on her. He had seen a great deal in the last months and survived events that had changed him irrevocably. He did not insist upon answers from the woman sitting grave and silent in his study.

He was not quite past wonder; he was yet ready and prepared to be once more afraid. Therefore, much wiser than he had been in the past, he saw her out. His return to the study saw him quickly refresh the teapot – and furiously set to work.

Alone, Abby had returned to the Hythe home on the hill.

Today, again alone, she had walked to the study, poured a glass of brandy, and downed it. Then she had gone to the desk and retrieved what Cass had entrusted to her, a prize and a memento of his journey into darkness and death. Glittering, like a crystal marble, scattering light across the room – the Orb was once more in her hand.

The Orb – the Eye of the First Gryphon – relic, symbol – weapon?

It came to Cass for a reason.

Alesia carried it with her, through death, to her own crypt – for Cass to recover here, in this time.

From the line of Fitzalan – and Ava is of that line.

And that line is long.

In her hand, the Orb had suddenly warmed and grown bright, and the walls, with their wide shelves heavy with books, with the quaint rug and family portraits – all faded from Abby's sight.

Instead, she stood in a strange room – beyond lay a wide bed, one whose linens lay tumbled, and yet the wand on their white counterpane still gleamed, both threat and promise. She looked down – at her feet was a knife or dagger, intricately wrought, its blade sharp and drenched in fresh blood. Beside it was a book, its leather bindings were immeasurably old, gilt and girt in gold. Its lock shivered into awful life under her glance – and the book opened to her avid gaze.

Pages turned; the images of drowned cities, of burning spires, of tottering buildings and shattered lives passed swiftly before her eyes – and the dark runes on those pages grew bright, bright with mayhem and with blood. Pages opened into yet more pages – and more books appeared – and in each, their message and portent was dark and full of doom.

Now pain assailed her, fear gripped her suddenly for without warning the light in the Orb collapsed and the crystal went cold in her hand – and with the chill in both heart and hand had come the voice.

Come.

No more than a whisper; it was as if the breeze had stolen past the open window, setting into motion the curtain. Like a hand that lightly raked its nails across a line of text, and fixed upon a single word, a sound came – one that stayed in the mind.

Come.

Abigail Hythe had risen from her chair.

The Orb had gone into a locked drawer. Then she had moved closer to the doors that opened onto the gardens. So here she now stood, and as a storm from the south reeled high overhead, she looked out beyond the French doors to the brick lined walks that crossed the grounds, that divided the parterres into boxes, pulling a walker's passage ever higher, ever deeper into copses, trees and shrubs.

Away from safety.

As is the case in every garden, however small and tame there is a boundary.

It is one that exists between the known world and one less predictable, less defined, less contained. It is a world far distant, in place and purpose from the sturdy wood and worked stone of habitation. It presides away from those structures – and the more spiritual constructs – that man erects as barriers against the dark.

The Hythe gardens had had long years to reach this pinnacle of depth, of complexity and beauty. And of mystery; for the family, while long tenants of this home at the top of Guild Down Road, had not been the first inhabitants, in either house or land. Long ago, in the past, a careful hand had laid the first stones here. That hand had set the location and position of the garden's lanes and paths, paths that radiated from a curious central circular nave – a knot garden – that lay at the very heart of the grounds.

Almost invisible from the house, that spot now seemed to glow in the scattered morning light. Now that early sun was eclipsed by sudden clouds that sent the house and land into cool, fleeting shadow.

Abby stood alone in the house.

Her hand reached out – slowly she opened the door – and stepped outside. Her gaze took in the wide expanse.

Come.

She stepped onto the walk. Across the mossy bricks, Abby made her way down the paths. Darker grew the path; shadows lengthened around the shrubs and the sky rumbled.

Come.

She walked through a labyrinth of green, bound yet not subjugated by ancient brick. Here, boxwoods and herbs flourished in rampant confinement. Abby's fingers brushed against their borders; scent rose, laden with the memories of the past, of times and lives long spent.

She had stopped at the very heart of the garden, of the maze – and waited.

It did not take long.

From the distance and for not only the woman in the knot garden – thunder had pealed low warning. Her gaze swept past the hedges, then stopped, riveted on the heavy foliage some thirty paces beyond – as that foliage began to move. There was no longer any time in her mind for wonder, only the rapid- fire course of her thoughts – and her fear.

Not possible.

How can it be 'Above'?

But it was; first came the eyes, as golden as Cass had described, and larger than those of any lion. The strange coat, with spots and stripes, that came next as the Cat freed its huge, uncanny head and slowly rose from cover. And as the monster moved closer – it grew, suddenly looming enormous as it seated itself on the cool, moss covered brick.

It gazed at the woman whose face was pale but whose voice was strong and rang with challenge.

"Damnéd Thing. What do you want."

The voice of the creature from Hell was sweet and resonant.

"Why, dear Lady, I want nothing, at least nothing I can speak of now. I am here to give you a message."

Abby's eyes flashed.

"From whom?"

"From Tam."

There was no time for anything now, not speech, not exclamation.

Abigail's face went white.

The demon cat leaped up, growing larger and larger with each bound. In a rush, it raced up to her, then crouched low at her feet.

Her last sight was of golden eyes, blazing exuberantly with chaos – as a massive paw swept up and across – and savage claws struck directly at her face.

CHAPTER 4

MIGHTIER THAN THE SWORD

*Damned Cat. Damned 'Underland'. Damned – all of it.
With the operative word being 'damned' …*

Just a short time ago, Quist had come to his
senses on the stone floor of the church, the golden
ring still clutched in his hand. From there it had gone
into his pocket, where it had been promptly
forgotten. Now he sat at the Hythe house with his
mind full of questions – and his heart full of wrath.
There was nothing for it; with a remarkably steady
grip considering the recent events, Montgomery Quist
again took up the treasure that might or might not
have saved his life – and studied it more carefully.

There had simply been no time before; there
was considerably less now, although neither he, Cass
nor Abby were yet aware of this. They were, however,
deeply grateful for one another's presence and the
illusion of comparative safety – if only for the
moment. For the nonce, neither Cass nor Quist had
breathed much more than a word about the
Professor's own recent intimate meeting with a
demon in a haunted church.

Now Quist's eyes glowed as he expounded.

"There are indeed letters. My word – just imagine, Old Frisian, possibly a drop of Futhark, although I can't say Elder or Younger."

Cass smiled for the first time in hours – the man's sheer resilience, his pure enthusiasm after so nearly having reached a grisly end just moments before simultaneously stunned and reassured him. But it was a grim smile; had the Mage looked up he would have found Abby's gaze bright upon him. Quist had barely blinked as Cass' eyes had widened at the sight of the circle of gold. But the Mage had grown pensive. He had held the ring for no more than a moment and for that moment, Monty half imagined that the Sorcerer would put it on. That thought somehow sent a ripple of disquiet through the scholar and he was inexplicably relieved when Cass returned it to him with a low murmur.

"Keep it safe – keep it secret."

The moment passed and Quist's lips had moved as, once again, blessed habit took precedence over recent calamity.

"Whatever the meaning here, the message is short. See how the letters curve – and here. A name perhaps? Or a brief message – but we will know soon enough. Yes, I will want to look into these. It might be serious, I think. Yes, quite serious, unless I am very much mistaken."

Quist turned to Abby. "My dear, would you hold onto this for me – just for a bit? I shall be going home to rest."

Abby took the ring as Quist's warm gaze fastened on Cass, and he suddenly reached to take hold of the young man's arm. The Professor then scooped Abigail Hythe into a sturdy embrace; a profound and meaningful silence united the three. Light-hearted professions of hope were passed all around, and Quist left.

He did not mention where he was going next or what he intended to do there – nor what he had had kept hidden in his pockets since early that day, and had retained all throughout the attack on his life.

Cass showed him out; he was no longer smiling.

Quite serious, indeed.
It's all too serious, all too familiar.
Again.

Just hours before, driven by an urge too powerful to resist, the Mage had burst into a notoriously historic nave to find Quist collapsed on the cold pavers before an ancient, ruined altar stone.

When Cass had pulled up to find Quist's battered classic auto with its owner nowhere in sight, the Mage's alarm became palpable fear. He had expected the worst; instead, Quist had soon roused – and the enormous paw print in the sand of the crypt was all the explanation that Cass needed.

33

By then the rain had stopped; scant but infinitely sweet sunlight lay dappled across an excavation site all too familiar to both himself and the one on the stones.

That ride back to Guildford, to find Abby bloody and shaken in her study was as nightmarish as the almost certain events that had not been revealed by Abigail Hythe, as all three had steadied themselves over brandy.

The horror had left; doubt and dread remained. Cass was left alone with his aunt; her smile was warm but weak, and the Mage marveled once again at the simple strength and courage of the two.

They have faced much – with me, because of me – for some time. And to face that nightmare, unarmed …

Cass turned to his aunt, in dispute as much by what Abby hadn't divulged as by what she had. While Abby had spoken, he and Quist had exchanged many a look.

As close a call as Quist. That monster more than once terrified me – yet here she sits, calm, centred – and curiously purposeful. And we both felt something …

For the sight of an apparently unassuming gold ring on a man's palm had brought a quick intake of breath, and a flush to the woman's cheek. Abby had stiffened in her chair but had said nothing.

Now she faced him and studied him gravely.

"Tell me – what *else* did Monty find – at the site?"

He was thunderstruck; slowly, carefully, he informed his aunt she had not been the sole target. There would be no opportunity for comment.

Abby had sprung to her feet.

For nearly a minute she had paced while her nephew wondered how and from where she had found the strength – blood still oozed from the wounds left by the Cat.

Then she sent him upstairs; he took those stairs two at a time, returning with the slip of parchment taken from the little bay room in Iain Fitzalan's home. At the desk, Cass lowered the lights as his aunt took up the narrow band of ancient hide. It was true parchment, light, and creamy and soft; in her hand its surface shone, as smooth and blank as when the Mage had recovered it.

"It was *behind* Alesia's sword, you say?"

He nodded.

"As I said; it could only have been deliberately concealed there."

He waited. Again, she studied the thing; he'd watched her do this before – darkness alone could give life to the message on the sheet – and Cass wondered.

Why this urgency, why do this again, now?
What is it she's looking for now?

She moved the parchment into shadow; the words sprang into sight – but to the Mage, they seemed darker, clearer, more insistent than ever

35

before and Abby studied that clamorous message with an intensity he had not seen before, as if the attack in the garden had brought a new, terrible meaning – to her alone.

It came to him as a shock, as a revelation – realisation – and he was seeing it for the first time.

How is it I never got an answer to that question – to all the other questions – that I somehow was unable to ask?

In the blinding light of sudden vision, Cass went over in his mind – the countless observations, all the conversations he had had with Abby – particularly about wands, and swords and closed time loops and threads.

Every time, the actual basis of events had been masked – and I did not question.

How is it that Abby has been able to do what she does – what now I see what she has always done? And her wand – left to her by Fitzalan – is it the wand or the woman?

As if she had heard him, she looked up at him suddenly. It came to him like a thunderbolt that someone – or something – had forestalled any of the questions he should logically have been asking, now and before – about a great many things.

Yet now – I see – I am suddenly freed.
Why? And who has released me from this spell?

A young man who had repeatedly resisted the gift of power granted to him smiled now; the spell had indeed been perfect, for he had never seen it, had never recalled not having questioned at all.

That speaks power, and a prodigious one at that.

But now the enchantment is broken – now I see and I am free to ask – and now I see even more clearly that for now, I must forebear, for urgency cries out against reason – and I must act.

Her eyes were still upon him and she held him with her gaze.

"In the past, in the Thoth deck, do not forget – the Brothers are also the Lovers. 'With Wands is marked the Page', Cass. At the Silent Pool – the Elemental spoke to you."

"Yes, the Undine. But …"

"Two things are important now – first you must leave immediately – you needed to call Percy; do so now. See – and act. Secondly – remember Her words – and the warning. *Remember.*"

The sound of her voice, the edge of fear, of desperation, compelled him. His phone was in his hand; he waited as empty air added to an already growing sense of alarm.

"He's not picking up."

Abby regarded him.

"You'd better go."

"I will. And *you*, are you sure that you're …"

"I am. Go."

Abby nodded. She was still pale but her eyes shone in a way Cass hadn't seen before and he was unexpectedly struck, for her gaze was like that of someone else, familiar but as yet unplaced.

The sun was beginning its slow march westward as Cass' car sped along a road darkening under the limbs of tall, looming trees.

But his mind was miles away; Abby had opened a scarcely healed wound.

In his mind, he was back in a savage past, standing again before a haunted Pool, under a bright moon. With a bit of stone glittering in his hand – he had watched as the runes there grew brighter than the lunar disk above him – and an *entity* had risen from the choking weeds, risen freed. No longer bound, the Undine had transfixed him with the sight of Her true face – Her unspeakable power.

The Undine – born of mist, of immemorial ocean – of the union of heaven and flood … Rose before me…

And I had worked the rite …

He had not worked it alone.

He could but wonder – had the warrior beside him that night shared that vision of Heaven – and Hell?

It was the name of the Master – that, coupled with the shard and me, myself – and the force of the girl beside me.

He had looked straight into the Undine's eyes.

There he had seen such desire, such blood lust that he had stood in ecstasy, in wonder and terror – for She had called to him, wordlessly, spirit to spirit, as could no mortal woman. The Mage had told no one of this, how Her words had broken over him, conquered him as surely as the terrible flood She had finally unleashed in the mere.

At Her rising, the living air once again took the form of Her song, and that song has never left my heart for a moment.

She calls me – and Her words haunt my dreams – 'Lest Brother mar what Brother hold … A Prince shall rise … Beware His book'…

And now – with Wands is marked the Page … the Book … the Page.

The Brothers are also the Lovers …

He was close to Onslow's studio now; as he made the last turn, he again tried to reach the man – and the call went through.

"Percy. Percy?"

To Cass' horror, all he heard was the clash of combat – and a veritable tumult of crashing. All Cass could think of was the Cat – and its savage claws. This sent him into such a frenzy of haste that he nearly drove the car onto the curb. The vehicle slammed to a halt and Cass raced to Percy's door.

There came no answer to the bell or his fist hammering frantically on the door. Instead, he was jarred into action – from deep within the house came again the sounds of chaos.

He did not hesitate; the side window splintered under his blow and he leapt into the house running to the floor below, always in the direction of tumult. He flew down the stairs – and went full into the arms of an assailant with a drawn blade – who promptly threw him to the floor.

In the near dark, overturned chairs and scattered rugs marked the lower studio; Percy only used this for special training. Cass was alone with his attacker; there was no sign of the master anywhere. There was enough light to see the weapons arrayed on the walls – Cass snatched up the nearest blade and went for the figure that feinted, then suddenly leapt at him again.

"You can't win this! Stand down!" exclaimed the Mage.

A low laugh reached his ears as the one before him redoubled the assault, launching such a fury of expert blows that Cass found himself in full retreat – and suddenly sprawled on the floor, with his sword raised high in desperation.

The lights flashed on.

"This is something I'd have paid a great deal to see!" laughed Percy Onslow – and Cass looked in astonishment as the sword master advanced.

As Percy came forward, a figure stepped into view from behind him; here was the one whose skill had landed him on his knees.

It was a girl – she wore full gauntlets and body armour of worked leather, and her dark eyes shone with some concern – but more delight.

She came near, pulled off her gloves, and hauled the Mage to his feet as Percy dusted him off.

Onslow grinned again as his gaze went from one to the other with satisfaction, then he turned to the Mage.

"Cass, I'd like you to meet Pen – my niece."

CHAPTER 5

A MAP AND A MERE

The Devil take it!

I have every right to act the Fool.

I'm old enough to have earned it. Well, not quite.

The tirade, not quite silent for it was not entirely under Quist's breath, was soon over.

He stood a scant half dozen miles from the site of his own near demise. The autumn colour was just beginning to feel its way across the bracken and into the forest glades around Shere.

The car park was deserted; he took that for a sign. He also took one last glance at his map – and halted.

My word – how did I not see that before?

Before his eyes, in the clear light of day – this day, right here – the small design at the map's lower left corner seemed somehow different.

Not different – clearer, much clearer – for surely there is a small compass rose right there.

A compass rose …a rose …

Whatever can that mean?

Puzzled, driven on, he returned the fragile parchment to his pocket. His hand went over that pocket, patting it with a sense of comfort. Then he readied a story, one that would likely satisfy any steward of the reserve, should one be encountered.

I believe I shall be free to go as I please.

It was a rare instance of relief; he counted on the fact that funds for both public servants and the rangers of Guildford's Surrey Trust had been slashed. Alone he was now, and alone he continued, crossing the pavement, heading for the trees.

This determination of going as he pleased was an unique reaction against recent events. He was grateful to be still standing, still alive; the Cat could so easily have killed him.

It spared the potential messenger; how fortunate I was to serve as the carrier of dark missives for my friends.

The shreds of his fear had found new life in a curious bravado, one he scarcely recalled having had ever before. The Professor felt decades younger, chock-full of righteous indignation.

Perhaps that's how its done – you are threatened with death, you become incensed – and that's all that's needed to begin the quest. So are heroes made if not born.

He had not added vengeance to that list; it was new to him at his age.

The nerve of that Thing – threatening me – and Abby – I wonder what made it stop?

His indignation, his curiosity, his sudden list toward the hero's heading, these were all likely to get him killed. Yet, Montgomery Quist was not just a man of vast experience, for his was a spirit deep in

44

canny acumen. He was ultimately an immensely practical man; he looked after life and limb and intended to part gracefully with neither.

And I can be bloody mean in a fight.

After all, I am not just an archaeologist – I am tenured.

He had learned a variety of new skills, just in the last months.

Casually, yet with the consummate care that only a man anticipating trouble can put forth, he stepped from the car park, and left the modern world behind. In too short a time, one rife with starting at shifting shadows and snapping twigs, he stood before what had been a slight blue stain on a centuries- old guide, but remained a contemporary marvel.

Notorious in legend, and most certainly in fact, for now I know the truth of this place – the Silent Pool.

It had been many years since he had stood here. Those years had seen changes in man and mien; drought, loss of trees, and to many outside the local area, the slow, inevitable decline into obscurity. Yet, lovely still were the green banks and deep shadows of overhanging limbs of this place, whose lineage was contemporary with the line of kings, whose legends still rang with the dim, sweet chords of ancient magic.

To the scholar at the edge of the mere, this place signified much more.

The tales of King John, of the drowned maiden – now, they mean nothing.

For a very singular young man had informed this scholar not just of a journey, but one that had brought that young man to stand very nearly where Quist himself now stood. Cass had revealed how the legend had sprung to life.

Is She there still?

That Elemental, who lay bound and helpless until Cass freed Her?

Or has She fled this modern age? Is this soft language of bird and wind and water – all that remains of the lingering song of that One who guides the seas, whose soul is the essence of water in all its forms – in all its power – everywhere?

Freed was the Undine – and the shard that Cass found, that made a circuit round past and present, had somehow played a part.

From a pocket inside his jacket – he pulled the plaster copy of that same shard Cass had taken across time.

And enterprising and reckless of danger, Montgomery Quist stood at the edge of a mere with the image of a stone engraved with runes – and waited, waited against the chill of the coming dusk, with his shoes wet amongst the rushes, and a gnat or two caught in his white hair.

A half hour crept by.

His hopes – and fears – were dashed.

There's nothing.

Ah well, we are not all Sorcerers.

We are merely scientists. We are not of the line of Fitzalan, nor even a terribly persuasive man …

He turned away – and his breath caught in his throat.

Not long ago, he had stood in Fitzalan's library, overcome by a growing sensation very like the one that crept slowly, yet imperiously over him now.

I see nothing, feel nothing but a curious stillness descending – yet I feel somehow no longer alone.

It was true.

As if suddenly aware of the man's presence, the voices of bird and wind fell to silence. Quist turned back to face the slip of emerald water before him; light sparkled and small ripples skated across the Pool's centre. The rest was shadowed trees, glades, and shrubs pressing close and secretively about the long stretch of the mere.

Overlaid with its majestic symbols, the shard was in his hand.

Now, moved by an indefinable impulse, he held out that relic, and knelt beside the mere. Then, for no reason other than that of a sudden deep wave of spirit, of homage to this spot and all that it had seen throughout the vastness of centuries – he wet the stone in his hand with the clear, cool waters of this wondrous place.

A shock – as of something exploding deep in the mud of the Pool resonated about him and ripples coursed across the mere's surface. From that surface, mist began to form, to rise, as if the mere were boiling just below.

The waters slowly began to swirl – then to foam.

The sky above had darkened unaccountably.

Over the head of the now terrified scientist echoes of thunder rolled – and for a second, sleet raked unaccountably across the ground at his feet.

What in blazes ….

His voice stuck in his throat.

For stunned, he watched as a solid mass of water bubbled up from the very centre of the mere.

A roiling bore of water lifted and began to surge forward, to the very limits of the dell – and without thinking, possessed by a mounting fear of he knew not what – Quist hurled the shard directly at the crest of the high wave that seemed determined to bear down upon him.

Impossibly, as if alive, the water bounded up – higher – ready – reaching – and clear, frigid fingers enveloped the shard, as a single pillar of deep green formed out of the chaos at the mere's centre – and to the scholar's unblinking gaze came a sight he would take with him to the grave.

There were eyes in the pillar, as green and blue as the waters of every ocean.

The sound of endless voracious waves pounding across countless, building and devouring unknown shores deafened the man beside the Pool.

Those eyes, wide and brilliant looked out – seeking – and they fixed upon Montgomery Quist. And he stood there, barely under his own power now, a mortal whose nostrils were assailed by the scent of salt spray, whose mind reeled with the roar of water, thunderous and numbing – and everywhere was the melody of the open seas, whose reach is limitless, whose waves rise and fall stories high, eternal, unstoppable – immortal. He was there, rapt, in the glory and wrath of eternal ocean, helpless and desiring nothing more than to be one with it, with the power and ferocious soul of the great sea …

Like a clap of doom, thunder sounded right over his head – and the spell was broken.

Quist found himself on his knees in the mud.

He looked down and cried out – there before him half hidden in the soft dark wet came the glint of gold – solid gold – and his shaking hand stretched out to it.

The bore had dropped to a simple wave, low and innocuous. It quickly receded back to the Pool's centre, leaving one mortal man wordless, in homage, a man who for one moment had hovered at the verge of madness, of ecstasy – as had one other, far younger man, one no longer truly young in any ways our sterile world might offer him.

Quist was breathing hard; in his hand, he gripped something unfathomable, small, curved, tarnished and green, cast and worked in marvelous metals.

He barely felt it.

And all he could think of was the vision of what had passed, one of incomparable violence and beauty, both primitive and majestic, one that had touched him only lightly with dark, incomprehensible dominion.

I have seen Her — yet what I saw was only a part, and I am yet amazed — and still alive.

I am amazed at Caspian Hythe, at his strength, his sheer courage — to have faced Her — for I feel that the veil — the wall — between us was weak, puny to the point of my own demise.

Merciful Heavens — this is what She is, what he has seen and known — and yet survived. This is what he had seen — and felt — when She rises …

The last evidence of aberrant water was gone; the surface of the Pool was as before, smooth and quiet. And the sounds of life — of wholesome, living things unsullied, untouched by sorcery, yet somehow steadfast in sovereignty to the primal Elemental he had just glimpsed — those sounds came slowly back.

Feeling both unutterably blessed and cursed, Quist rose to shaking feet — and pulled his phone from a drenched and mud smeared pocket.

CHAPTER 6

REMEMBER ME

Cass rose to his feet.

Time had passed since he had received Quist's stammering summons.

Even more time, both natural and not had passed since he had last stood here on these shores.

Seeing the place again through the eyes of past trial, of past awe, the Mage stood silent and thoughtful. The Pool spread cool and quiet before him; in ready anticipation of the coming dark, shadows now made stronger inroads, creeping steadily up and out from the low hanging trees.

The call from Quist had only interrupted two; in Percy's studio, Onslow's niece had replaced her weapon, offered up the requisite courtesy, warmly shaken hands with the one she had assumed was her uncle's pupil – oh, had she only known – and left.

Percy had carefully closed the door on the girl and turned a sober eye on that 'pupil'.

"Have you seen the papers?"

Cass had swept up the issue offered by his friend; the article was on the second page, where only the two in the room, and perhaps a handful of significant others might have found interest – and more.

Couched in the common vernacular of yet one more report of increasingly frequent random violence, this piece was different and Cass' eyes widened as he read.

He put the paper down.

"When was he found?"

"This morning – *where* may be more to the point."

"I saw; up near the Mount."

"Apparently, he'd been loitering about the grounds for a week or so. Drunk usually, sleeping under the roadway."

For Cass, it was simply another message – brutal, mocking, a demand for attention.

"Apparently—something took notice," he said.

"Apparently. He died of his wounds. I made the call down to the hospital; the coroner's a good friend. What it doesn't say here may be of interest – he was torn open, Cass. One leg was gone. His head was missing, as was his heart – it was pulled clean out of his chest."

The fight master had been steadily regarding the Mage; Cass had made no response. His silence chilled Percy Onslow.

"The police are withholding information. They don't want a panic. They are at a loss to explain the nature of the attack – how the wounds were inflicted – and by what. Are we equally at a loss?"

Now Cass faced him; his voice was low.

"No."

The Mage turned away and his eyes went to the wall where Onslow's weapons ranged. Their naked blades shone brightly – invitingly – in the dusk.

They were all live blades; one of the finest – and the favourite of the young man – seemed to call to him from afar. Cass turned back.

"Percy. Something has risen – from *'Below'* – *and it is not the Gryphon.*"

Onslow's jaw set. It was then that Cass' phone had rung. Cass had listened hard, uttered a low affirmative and his eyes had been bright when he next met Percy's gaze.

"You're with me."

Percy had stood long, gazing at the water's edge of the Silent Pool – listening as Quist described the monumental occurrence of the last hour.

The swordsman had come forward when the scholar – clearly, but in a voice still tainted with fear – described the pillar of water coming to life before his eyes.

"Monty, I cannot forbear …"

"Percy, I cannot blame you! It sounds madness – on my life, I haven't had a drink. I could use one now – but with these eyes I saw Her – the

Undine rose before me and it was She, undoubtedly She – that brought this thing out of the mud and into my hands."

Percy turned to Cass.

The Mage walked closer to the line of reed-choked green that skirted the Pool.

There he stood, silent, with ripples of clear water just caressing his boots.

He seemed miles away from them; Quist would have said centuries away.

Cass' face was expressionless as his hand stretched out, reaching over the waters of the mere – and Percy watched thunderstruck as what could only be a figment of his imagination loomed into life.

The light over the Pool changed, suddenly softer, more radiant – the shadows under the trees deepened. And the scent of the water – somehow, it was like no water that the sword master had ever experienced before. That scent cooled and refreshed, it was vibrant with hidden life, and for an instant, Percy was unsure of where he stood – or when.

For the breeze quickened – the softest of winds curled about the Mage, lifting his hair – and the water at his feet whirled in a maze of liquid circles, a passion of brilliant movement, movement inexplicable but undeniable to both Quist and the sword master.

Slowly, Cass knelt; reverently, calmly, his hand dipped into the water at his feet – and all went to quiet. He rose to his feet and walked away from them, away from the Pool.

The scholar had shared a hard look with the man of the sword; he gripped Percy's arm – and nodded meaningfully.

Percy did not demur.

The time for doubt had passed – silent, bewildered, they followed Caspian Hythe away from the haunted mere.

It had taken little time for them to convene at the Hythe residence. Onslow was still nonplussed by what he had seen and heard, not just from Cass weeks before but by Quist's narrative. As for what he himself had witnessed – experienced – at the Pool, he had no words.

I have no grounds, no footing in this.

To have saved Caspian Hythe not once but twice – virtually bringing him back from dead – and to have the Elemental, the Thing still here – in my own present, in my lifetime – just miles from the place I have called home – that is beyond imagining.

What Quist had taken from the Pool was now once more on dry land; Abby turned it over in her hands.

Some of the remnants of its long sojourn under sand and water had been removed. Brightly now, like new, did little bits of the ancient gold send enthusiastic rainbows about the study.

The thing fit across her palm.

55

It was a semi-circle of worked, time-encrusted gold; queer markings as of letters lay etched into its surface on both sides. The etchings held their own luster.

"Silver," murmured Monty. "Or something far more dear. And it is old, Cass. I cannot place it anywhere nearer than a millennium. Regardless of the place it holds in our mystery – a priceless find – we must plumb its secrets – and soon."

They had all regarded the scholar then, for his voice had lowered as if he might be overheard, and not by them. He glanced up; his gaze was stern – and fearful. That gaze fixed on Cass. It was the same bright if troubled gaze that had met Cass when he and Percy arrived at the Pool.

Yet here Quist was again, with Cass and Abby, now ever so much more determined, for he believed he saw a pattern.

"I believe this has come to us now, for a reason. You see, I believe it will solve riddles – at the very least, the one you discovered in Iain's library and let us not forget that map. This little bit of gold is a connection, a link in a train of events that has led from somewhere far away, and long ago – to now, to the appearance of that dreadful Cat – the servant of the Black Queen – *'Above'*. This relic found its way to us for a reason. So did the Cat."

Cass came forward and picked up the little arc of brilliance, holding it for only a moment. Yet, for that moment – the light in the study seemed to dim. It was a slight change – but all looked up, all marked it – and the Mage put the relic down before his aunt.

The nephew regarded the aunt; Abby was white.

"Abby."

She faced him.

"Who is Tam?"

She exhaled mightily; then profound silence held sway.

She went to him and touched his face.

Abigail Hythe then walked to the mantel. There, photos paraded across the heavy wood. She picked up one – it was of Iain Fitzalan and she gazed upon it in silence as Cass continued.

"Monty is right. The Cat came here – directly, *deliberately* – to confront you. Why *you*, Abby?"

She replaced Iain's portrait.

Percy refreshed his glass and brought one to Abby; she took it and walked away from Onslow, from them all as Percy's voice rang in the room.

"That's easy; the Thing knows you care about her, Cass. Because she is your aunt; there's a threat there. That's a given."

"No."

The word floated from across the room. Abby's voice was low; shocked silence descended again. She turned to face them.

"No, Percy, it isn't a given. And I'm afraid your observation is only half right."

"Whatever are you saying, Abigail?" asked Monty.

She stood tall and straight; her voice was as steely as the look she gave to all.

"I can only hope that I am as dear to Cass, as he is to me. And yes, that creature's determination to single me out has to do with *blood*, or very much more to do with it than you may imagine. Yes, I am a threat – and also a liability."

Unexpectedly she went to Cass.

"My dearest Caspian, I have watched you grow up. I watched as your father entrusted more and more of his confidence in your care – to me. I watched as you lost first one, then the other of your natural kin. I have loved you well – for many years. But – and hear me now, most closely – regardless of what you and many more have thought – *I am not your aunt.*"

Stunned beyond words by the revelations of the last hours, Caspian Hythe paced the garden behind the house.

His troubled walk took him into and out of the shadows of dusk; his mood was one of extremes, as mercurial as the light and darkness that set the garden's green avenues into piebald inscrutability.

He was barely aware of the contours of the moss embellished brick path beneath his feet; a feather might have brought him to the ground.

Convoluted; cursedly convoluted; not unexpected, but now clear – clear at last.

A woman whose lineage, whose relationship to his father – to himself – he had never questioned; too late now came the tally of little things. There it stood, the evidence, the indictments, countless episodes where the true nature of Abigail Hythe's history might have been suggested, if not betrayed outright.

Her taking leave when I was quite small – when my mother had nothing but the most plausible reasons for an absence which could only have been inexplicable – if only to me.

So the charade began.

So young; when Abby might have been with us, to help with me, the new child – and my birth had been a hard one, as both my health and my mother's have attested to all our lives since.

Where had Abby been when the man professed to be her brother and only kin – might have needed her most?

She had been busy with a birth of another kind.

The pieces were now in place, the whole mocking him in its simplicity, its completeness – its sudden, and very real implications.

Tam – the only natural child of Abigail … whom?

That baby had been given up, but not by Abigail Hythe – not by the sister of Randolph Hythe.

That child was given up by Abigail Fitzalan.

The curious gift of a wand from a dead man's estate – the close attention Abby paid to Ava that first night at supper, that meeting only divulged to Cass when he and the red-haired beauty had passed – with warning – *'Below'*.

Now clear was the reason for Abby's curiosity about Ava's birth date – what a surprise it must have been to have the daughter of Iain Fitzalan in the house that Abby had inherited from the Hythe family – a young woman of the closest blood relation possible.

Except for one.

The shock was lessening by the second.

Abby had always had the gift – for the cards – and ultimately – for an unknown craft – not only all my life but especially now, at the part of this story that I only just entered – by accident.

Yet all is as she said – as the Master had said – there are no accidents.

The shock had not been his alone; Abby's confession had rendered her friends speechless.

There had come only a look from Cass – for the lady before them had already suffered a great shock – then Monty, ever the consummate gentleman – had overcome his need to know all, all at once. Rising swiftly he had gone to the woman standing

60

pale and alone, and taking both her hands in his, had kissed her forehead.

"My dear friend; Randolph Hythe was a great man. Right now, his son stands there. His sister –the sister of Randolph Hythe, in *spirit* if not in *fact* – I hold in my hands. *Right now*. Let us stay with that and nothing more – *right now*. We all have far too many questions, too many fears, to unravel, to explain away. So I think I speak for all. Rest; grow strong, even stronger – grow mighty – as you have always been. We all stand with you, in allegiance – in strength – in the highest regard."

Quist looked about him.

"That said, we must all be on our guard now, from any quarter. Govern the time carefully; we can ill afford to waste any."

While Cass meditated what new havoc the Cat might be planning, and Percy mentally did inventory of his store of weapons, Quist came to stand over the bit of metal that somehow both compelled and warned in its unholy brilliance.

As if now loathe to touch the thing he halted, then quickly found paper at the desk and expertly completed a rubbing of the designs on both its surfaces. He picked up the artefact – and turned unexpectedly to Percy.

"Onslow, old man – you are clever with so many sharp and intimidating tools – for now they must be considered nothing less – may I entrust this thing to you? Will you keep it safe for a bit?"

He had not asked Cass or Abby to serve as guardian; this was not lost on any.

The past weighed on each, in vastly different ways. For had not Cass' father made a similar request of the sword master, and had he not kept safe – and secret – a canny and dangerous blade until an heir and rightful owner would appear to claim it?

Onslow took the thing and tucked it into his kit.

"I shall keep you apprised," he said.

The men had departed. Cass, wordless had held Abby close.

"Brandy – then bed. Whomever you are – dear to me, beyond price."

Abby had laughed; the old sparkle was back, one that reminded the Mage so clearly of Fitzalan himself when that one had been confronted by mortal adversity and immortal choice. Then the lady left; Cass remained, a true orphan in actual fact – to reconstruct his life – to ponder how it had come to be that his father had helped, nay perpetrated a sleight of hand, a shadow play that led to the creation of a new person.

A covert person, for that is what she was then and is now. Dad did this to protect her – from what? From whom?

His reverie was dark – the Cat – the Queen – and Tam – all set up camp in a conscience suddenly beset, uneasy past description. He stood now poorer by one aunt – and richer by far – having with him the sister of a man he had loved and lost – Iain Fitzalan.

And what of Ava Fitzalan – what of Ava, indeed.

His lonely circuit of the gardens was finished.

Potent night descended, claiming the earth and air, bringing with it a bracing coolness, one that rose from the ground and grass, reaching to succor, to enervate him.

The sky and land became dark and silent – and welcoming.

Night drew close over him as he left the grounds, turning his steps out and away, into the streets. Those steps took him back to a place familiar and sorrowful, the street of the Fitzalan family home.

As might the feet of any predator – any restless spirit – countless times since he had regained the world *'Above'* the Mage's steps had dogged this street.

Reliving endless scenarios, determined in hope, he had paused before the edifice. Night after night, in cheerful counterfeit, the lights had glowed out from the vacant dwelling. Day after day, the empty rooms had declared their privation.

Time after time – with a heavy, unforgiving heart he had departed, his vigil unending, his hunger unappeased. So it was that once more he stood before the home.

Except – this time …
Dear Heaven, what now?

There were no lights on in the house – not a one.

Practicality dictated the likelihood that the timer had gone awry. Overcoming his surprise, he made his way up the long walk to the door. So often had he made this place his haunt, that not a single neighbor stirred, no one in the homes beside Fitzalan's house marked the Mage's passage as he used his key.

Within the atrium, he halted. His hand went to the switch – light flooded the hallway.

At the control panel, he made the requisite inquisition; that panel dutifully informed him that all was well.

Perplexed and now wary, he made a circuit; not a sound came from the many rooms. The ground floor was secure – and he began to wonder.

Why do I feel safe?

Considering its macabre sense of humour – by all rights, a Cat ought to have been here – with me.

But, there is nothing.

With a last long look about him, the Mage reset the timers and secured the doors behind him.

Within the structure light once again blazed merrily. With the stars brilliant overhead and an early fallen leaf underfoot, Caspian Hythe left behind him the house where Iain Fitzalan and Ava Fitzalan had once lived. Weary, still wondering, with his tired mind on everything, his attention nowhere, the Mage's thoughts and steps turned toward home.

Home is not always a place of safety.

When he had left the Hythe house, such had been his state that he had taken little notice of the streets around him – no notice whatever of the shadowed lane across the way.

Fate rarely rewards imprudence.

Had he but raised his eyes he might have glimpsed it – in the dark at the end of that lane – a bright regard, where a careful gaze had marked not only the Mage's passage – but those of his friends as well.

It was only later – much later – with the sliver of a crescent moon shining in the sky, long after the Sorcerer had gone to his own rest that the lights in the Fitzalan house could be seen to flicker – and one by one – would again be steadily extinguished.

CHAPTER 7

HOW DOTH
THE CROCODILE

"Must you be making that infernal racket?"

Over the young man's shoulder, across the room – and it was decidedly lucky for the young man that it was across the room and he did not take notice – there came a long moment of silence – deep and threatening.

It was momentary only; an instant later the crunch of teeth working their way through bone and flesh resumed. The Cat finished its repast then turned a brazen gaze on the one at the desk.

Slightly built; here was no Heracles.

Rather, the mien of the one bent over his work suggested a Perseus, or even a young Odysseus. He was not unlike these; tall, almost fair with the eyes of a voyager, a captain – a conqueror.

Such ran the demonic feline's thoughts.

Tam – for that was indeed the name of the one garnering the full attention of the damned creature – did not look up. Instead, he bent more fixedly over the old desk, whose wood had seen a fair number of odd elements already come across its surface.

None of them had been as odd or as potentially significant as these.

First was a parchment, eerily alike to the one that another young man, very similar in figure and mien had found in a deserted house not long ago. Unsurprisingly, the two shared a common source. Tam ran long fingers over the smooth surface of the paper; unlike the one taken by the Mage, no letters rose into sight.

Just beside the slim page from another time lay a thing of a different sort.

The lamp on the desk threw a golden halo of light, one that limned the scattered corruption of ages past with the sheen of gold. It was a miraculous colour, one as compelling, as bright, as the intent in the eyes of the creature across the room who, its toilette finished, would have smiled had its fearsome jaws been capable.

I smiled 'Below' – or grinned, depending on one's viewpoint.

Here, smiling is for them – mortals – before they fully comprehend how little of the game they control.

And in this instance, it is precious little.

It was cool for this autumn; the Cat stepped fastidiously over the leg bone on the floor. It was what was left of a man; he would not be missed. The Thing sat beside the fire grate; it reveled in its new senses, so different from those it had had before. The world it had sported in before had been magnificent – in scope, in amusement.

But confinement only serves to whet the appetite; here, the Cat's powers, while not boundless, were still of a magnitude, one that set its whiskers trembling with anticipation.

Long was I chained; long have I slept.
Now I am awake – and ready for pleasure.
And my hunger is profound.

The Cat's last memory of its own demise still lingered in the creature's mind and sinister spirit.

For here, as *'Below'*, the primal elements of merciless violence, of the need, the hunger for blood, for chaos – these rightfully find their roots, their cause, their fuel – in the realm of spirit. In this case, they were nothing less than the font, the very word made flesh of the Thing in this room. That room remained mostly in shadow yet did the creature's keen vision pick out the many books, shelves of curios, the many token of this modern age.

With a glitter in his eye to match that of the relic on the desk, Tam examined the object yet again – the perfection of the arc, the letters and figures still obscured under time's incessant hands. The circle of metal was clearly incomplete – by the larger part.

Tam rose; the Cat watched hopefully.

"Is my help needed."

"No. Not yet."

Tam left the house while the Thing turned away and the tongue of a demon in feline form raked across the morsels still clinging to one man's final legacy.

From the cracks oozing merrily in the bone, a marvelous fragrance arose; a rumble came from the Cat's massive throat. It pondered with delight – and gratitude – the universal prevalence, the sheer impenetrability of mortal arrogance – and the universal certainty of its outcome.

Damn. And Damn again.

His house was quiet; the peace of a well guarded home proclaimed itself everywhere.

For some time now, Onslow had been happy here, captivated by Guildford's blend of old and new.

His house was older than most; the connection of this place to one of the world's finer authors had had little to do with Percy's choice to settle here. Lewis Carroll and his charming works held little charm and utterly no interest for a man whose military service had ended fortunately and swiftly – he'd taken no serious injury and had gleaned much in education – of survival skills and his own temperament. On the contrary, the impact of a life or death existence coupled with his mastery of it – and a good dose of luck, had combined to propel him into a new career, that of combat training.

One might expect that strife, fighting in any form would become anathema.

A surprise even for me; once I got a sword into my hand – all the pieces fell into place.

But Carroll – those mad worlds of words and fantasy – not a blip on my horizon, creative or otherwise.

All true – until this past year – when a mysterious sword entrusted to him by a dear friend had assumed the most monumental significance – when Caspian Hythe had appeared at his door.

He recalled the time when Cass had asked him if he missed the old days, of combat and campaigns. He had laughed, for he had – until he found Caspian Hythe.

To think, he wanted me to train him.

Little did I realise what Cass had already mastered – and at what cost – 'Below'.

What the father had only attempted – the son had accomplished.

And my life has never been the same.

Over a cup of strong coffee laced with brandy, his eyes roved over his collection – his tools – for he had come to understand that the spirit, the way, the ideology of the warrior far transcends the presence of a blade in the hand.

Surrounded by objects whose only true purpose – at least once upon a time – was to kill – he had learned, trained, practiced – he had been happy, he had been content.

Until now.

Now, as of just moments ago in the long age of the world – those blades are real again, they are weapons and capable of much more than the damage lent by a finely honed edge and firm intent.

Randolph's strange gift – that sword – bore runes for a purpose, one that would prove critical – in an entirely different age.

And who can say what role yet remains for them to serve – tomorrow?

How did it come to this?

How did it come – to me being in this?

He downed his drink and smiled.

The memory of his own kin bringing a warrior as prodigious as the Mage to the floor – that had been worth a lifetime of doubt. Cass had put up an exceptional fight; Pen had been outstanding. Percy was not a religious man and never one to readily ascribe any power to Fate. Yet the hair raised on his arm as he thanked the forces of Providence for his niece's lifelong fascination with weapons and for actual combat.

Curiouser and curiouser.

For now, she is here and she has met a singular fellow whose own skills are not confined to the use of a sword.

And I wonder …

He knew that Pen would make a fine historian; her academic work at Oxford in literature was progressive. Her promised return to visit again was nearly nigh; frankly, he awaited it eagerly. Percy Onslow was a natural loner; he was also a man ready and able to give of himself. Quite simply, he missed her; Pen's bright mind and honest enthusiasm was a pleasure and a compliment.

To me, to my passion – my creed.

So much of what I do, what I am, my own family has dismissed or denigrated.

But she has given substance to it – and to me.

She accepts me for what I've done, what I am. I have value to her – and hence, more to myself.

But now he was again embroiled in a mystery – in events that had turned unpredictably perilous.

He recalled the day Randolph Hythe had appeared on his doorstep with an unusual request. It had rained that day; there his friend had stood, with apologies – with a strangely pressing need.

And he had unwrapped a sword; its blade extraordinary, the workmanship unparalleled – and the lacy engraving of runes – and hearts – lay brilliant against the living steel.

Strange; how Fate turns on a dime, from past to present to future.

So it was with an understandable sense of trepidation that here he was again, once more in possession of a possibly dangerous artefact.

He pulled his chair closer to the worktable where blades and cloth, brushes and oil typically held dominion – and looked on something of another kind.

Perhaps not so different – the curvature is perfect – too perfect for such a man-made thing as ancient as Monty has suggested.

Man-made, very old …Can it be?

No, that's nonsense; I don't believe in aliens or any such interferences in our pitiful little world's events.

Yet, how clean the lines, how smooth and fine the workmanship …

Under his lamp, the markings were clearer.

A dab of oil, a rub, and the careful use of a soft brush across the arc and Onslow stared – and gasped. His regard grew intense, his observation more and more certain of the nature of the golden arc – and the sword master grew more and more alarmed.

Why – why should it alarm me – that this thing should suddenly be here?

Randolph's sword – went to his son, to Caspian Hythe – and he carried it into the past, a past that would resolve the road to death – for both Randolph, and for Iain Fitzalan … the road to death …

He turned away – had this not also come from what a scant year ago he would have described, scoffing – as a supernatural entity?

This came from Her – the Undine – why has She taken it from safety, and revealed it now – and it is clearly meant for Cass' eyes?

And for mine …

He rose and paced, speaking his thoughts aloud in his distress.

"If that is what I believe it is, *if it is* …"

"And what exactly – *do you believe it is*?"

The words came from behind him, from the doorway.

Percy whirled about.

Instinctively, his hand reached behind to seize the nearest weapon under it – a sword he had been restoring, a fine blade and one long enough to keep distance between himself – and the young man who stood barring the way out of the house.

Apparently unarmed, the fellow boldly sauntered in. His voice was melodious, familiar in some way to the man who now defiantly stood his ground with his back solidly flush against the table.

"Deception – and predation – it isn't love that makes the world go round, Mr. Onslow."

A profound silence was his only answer; Tam smiled.

"I notice you don't ask how I got in here. Or even my name."

Percy continued to maneuver slowly, carefully toward a drawer in the table.

"I've learned not to waste time on non-essentials. Please; feel free to leave now – in one piece."

"Oh, I have every intention of leaving. But we can be of use to one another first."

Percy's hand was on the drawer knob.

"I can't imagine what use you can have for me."

"Can't you? Don't bother; I think you'll find the gun is gone."

It was a dangerous turn in the scenario.

Yet Percy seemed unfazed – for he laughed lightly. Ever the master, he appraised the intruder, assessing age, musculature, balance and stance and the fluid movement Tam made to get closer to the table.

"Can't blame me for trying. What is it that you want, Tam? *Take it and go*."

Wide and brilliant were the young man's eyes.

A truly eerie glint shone out – one utterly devoid of anything remotely common to humanity and Percy Onslow, who had seen his friends and comrades torn and slaughtered in war, felt his blood go cold.

"How lovely," Tam murmured. "I'm not used to having the life offered to me – usually I have to take it, as you said. But – since you have offered …"

Percy knew the location and condition of every weapon in his care.

His hand had found the gladius and that was what he presented before him as his mind raced. Its focus was not on preserving his own life, but what he had left exposed on the table. So it was with deliberation that he moved, drawing Tam with him.

His attacker followed – as smoothly, as adroitly as another young man in his acquaintance.

And all the while, the announcement of the woman who had been Abigail Hythe stayed in his mind, pressing, like the point of a knife about to enter flesh.

Onslow sprang sideways – one hand lifted and toppled the worktable backward. It crashed down, and its bulk covered the arc of gold. Blades cascaded everywhere; Percy yanked up a dagger and Tam came up with a rapier – and sprang directly at the sword master. Where the youth learned his art was immaterial; with each stroke, each thrust, it was clear: he fought at a level that would soon over master the older fighter – and Tam fought to kill.

Youth gained over skill and strength – Tam's last swipe caught Onslow across his upper arm. The youth vaulted a chair thrown into his path – and cried out – in surprise and pain, for suddenly his own arm ran with blood and he stumbled – from nowhere, there was Pen, with her eyes on fire and a sword in her hand, attacking him without quarter.

She had entered soundlessly; she wasted no time.

Sword upon sword, the clash of metal against metal – Percy hung back, stupefied by the turn of events.

He hadn't heard her enter the house; clearly neither had Tam who yanked down a book case nearly on top of her. The chaos bought him the time he needed – Abigail's son was out the door in a breath.

Breast heaving, the girl stood for a moment more. Then she got Percy up onto his feet, and quickly bound his wound. Wary and well-trained, she secured the space then turned to him.

"So – *who was it that was so determined to kill you?*"

His silence was unnerving; she came close to him and made a vague gesture to the wall.

"Come now, uncle. If he were truly serious, *there's* the weapon he should have used."

Her levity went not so much unnoticed as ignored.

"Percy?"

Onslow took in a ragged breath.

He coughed once, then poured two glasses, and offered her one. He tossed down his own portion. Then, with consummate care, he went through the rubble in the room. Finally, he found and retrieved the relic from its spot on the floor.

With mounting alarm, the girl marked – how he handled the golden thing, the fear the man evidenced as he wiped its surface – as he hid it away in the drawer which no longer had any need of a gun. She reached for her phone.

"Don't," he warned.

Pen froze.

"It won't help, Pen."

His voice and face were dreadful. Slowly, she pocketed her device.

Onslow moved to sit stiffly on the only chair still standing. Pen came to him and knelt at his feet. She looked up at him, her face suddenly as pale as was his.

"Ok. You have *more* than my full attention. Slowly, carefully – tell me what the Hell is going on."

A man skilled in combat, both with the sword and with his bare hands, regarded his near kin. Bruised, bleeding – greatly humbled, still deeply shaken, that man struggled upon the edge of a blade, balanced for a seemingly eternal, agonising moment, between conscience and a sudden, fateful overwhelming sense of premonition.

Fate turned on its dime; the moment passed.

He went to the drawer, took out the relic, and placed it on the floor before his niece.

CHAPTER 8

WHY, OH WHY?

"Percy, why, oh why have you done this?"

His eyes went to Pen; she stood waiting just inside the Hythe door. Overhearing it, that nearly two third's condemnation in Abby's voice, the girl looked ready to bolt.

Abby waited; Percy needed no reminders – he was taking an enormous risk and he knew it. Cass' shock, when he took the sword master's call en route had set the tone. Now, the frank dissension in the voices rising in the Hythe study was all of a piece with it. Pen stepped further away, leaving the two together.

"Did he tell you, Abby?"

"Yes, Percy."

"She was *there* – when I desperately needed help; I'm only *here* because she was. More to the point, *Tam knows who she is*. She has the right to choose – and she can't do that unless she's here with us. I had to, Abby – I felt I had to. That's all."

The one who had been Abigail Hythe studied Percy's pale features. Then she positively beamed at him.

"Then I say, well done. Come."

When the Mage entered the study to the sight of Onslow's niece, his jaw set. Percy was filling in the details on the attack; when he finished, all the room, including the Sorcerer regarded the young woman with a different eye.

She knows; she knows too much, I'll warrant.
Yet will it secure her safety – or her death?

Percy came to Cass.

"I realize I had no right to divulge anything about you. But Caspian …

Percy broke off; he turned suddenly to Pen – and gestured to the Mage where he stood by the mantel.

"Pen. *Look at him.* Look at that man carefully."

To Cass' surprise, she walked straight to him – then studied his face with an intensity that both intrigued and abashed the Mage. His cheek coloured as Percy spoke again.

"Be honest; are you afraid of this man?"

There came a moment's hesitation.

"Weighing all you have taught me – against all I have heard – yes. I'd be a fool not to be."

All laughed – all except the Mage and he never took his eyes from her.

"That's not to say the rest of you are deficient in either sensibility or purpose. But, uncle, if what you've told me is true, and actually has happened – here is a power I don't understand. Nor is it a power I believe you or I, or anyone in this room can control – except for *him*. So, yes, I'd be stupid or damned crazy I weren't afraid of that man there."

That man there had never felt more alone, and less human.

He stood silent, amongst family and friends who would, without doubt, have laid down a life for him. But his difference, his solitude – it must have shown on his face, for Monty looked at Pen. Then he came forward – and stood before the Mage.

"Percy, it's a fine young lady you have there; I've no doubt she's even sharper than you are. Now, as to this; I may be a little crazy – no, don't smile Percy – or even a bit dim. But in the last few months, I've seen a great deal of *this man's* work. I may be still thunderstruck and stupid with awe; I may be in the dark as to what he *is* – and what he can *do*. I stand in that dark with more than one person in this room. *Someday, if we are damned lucky, or damned unlucky, if you will, we must all face the inexplicable – the eternal.* Because of *this man – I've had a glimpse of it.* So – no, speaking for myself, I'm not afraid of this man. I'm not afraid at all."

The fearsome one was overcome; his head lowered. Monty looked at the rest of them.

"There now; just so we're all on the same page, as it were. We all bring something to this, this *thing*, and this *quandary*."

83

He pulled out his map and set it on the table before them.

"I dare to suggest what I put *there* has come *here*, just now for a bloody good reason. I'm not superstitious. Yet I do believe things may be destined, fated if you will – to happen. Even if this is no different than the car that runs one over, out of the blue, on a fine day in May. It's happening – right now, to all of us. So that, there is yet more evidence of the inexplicable, and that's what I'm bringing."

Percy laughed – the sound of it was rich, and full of life and welcome in the room.

"Out of the blue on a fine day in May – if that doesn't aptly describe this, nothing does! Bless you Monty; none of us ever foresaw being face to face with a Hell Cat. And I for one am too old to ride a house over a rainbow – to land smack on an evil witch. But your point is well taken – *we should all be prepared to do so!*"

He took the golden arc from his kit and placed it beside the map and his voice was strange, charged with deep emotion for his eyes were on Cass.

"We've been through a lot, old man. And you—you have actually been through Hell and lived to tell of it. So let's all say here you stand, a little *inexplicable* today. But we're with you."

Cass looked from one to the next; his gaze stayed longest on Abby – she nodded and he went to the desk and retrieved the wondrous parchment he had found – been given – in Fitzalan's house. Carefully he laid it down beside the other two tokens – for they could be nothing less.

"Pen," said Cass. "Come here – if you're not too stupid – or damned crazy."

She drew near – the Mage's hands went over the parchment – the suddenness and starkness of shadow was enough; the girl gasped for the letters rose up into dreadful life.

There was not a sound in the room as she read – then she turned away.

Her face was flushed.

"Uncle – tell them what you told me."

He knelt down by the table, gingerly he picked up the piece of worked metal.

"*This* – nearly cost me my life – for whatever reason, I believe *this* is what Tam came to my house – to take. Look at it, Monty – come. In another moment, you'd have seen what it is – *what it could only be* – you see, I've been a voyager, too, in my time."

Quist looked, then stared, then gaped.

"Dear Heavens – now that it's cleaned – a sun – the moon – stars – planets – *is this some form of ancient Arabic?* Yes, Yes, Percy I see! *It's an astrolabe* – or part of one."

Pen's hand went across her forehead – she glanced at Cass' parchment, whose letters were already slipping into sleep – whose warning was already waning in the light.

"That bit of rhyme – a book, *a drownéd book* – there's only one book I can suggest that might be of interest to any here – *and to you, Cass, especially you – for you are already deep in it* – and also to my uncle's unwelcome guest – and now the pieces may begin to fit. A book of power – a myth, a legend or so I thought until now – and if it's real, my God – *it's beyond price*. It's from Shakespeare, his last most enigmatic work, *'The Tempest'* – could it be Prospero's book – a book of such power, such peril that a wizard – *a man perhaps modeled upon a real entity* – buried that book deep below the sea, beyond our reach, hid it God knows where?"

With extraordinary care, she picked up the astrolabe; it glittered like a captive star in her hand.

"The name of this thing, in Arabic – is *'Star Taker'* – it takes the path of the stars – and shows the way. *Is all of this connected, somehow, horribly linked – for us to see?* If so – God help us, God help us all. For it's just possible that this little bit of gold shows the way to where it lies."

Dead silence held sway.

Then – as one – the eyes of every person in the room went to Caspian Hythe.

CHAPTER 9

CATWALK

No man can be everywhere and everything at once. I know; I've tried. And I'm not just any man.

The defense didn't hold.

In raw desperation, on the pretext of needing air, the Mage had left them all behind at the house.

What are we to do?

What am I to do?

I don't need any more air. What I need is a miracle.

In a turmoil of indecision, he sought new perspective in isolation, more alone than ever before.

Utterly alone – use it – use it; don't waste it.

Look – and truly see.

Above, the moon freed itself from cloud, and light streamed over him. What the girl had said at the last – he still wrestled with it, stubbornly abjuring the certainty that his whole life, in both experience and knowledge, was of a piece with the one word that encompassed all.

Impossible.

The premise should be streaming somewhere on a cell phone. But, no – here it is right before us, in undeniable likelihood.

Had he not seen that Book, for it was the most extraordinary of volumes – in his mind, in dream too many times?

The verdigris on the lock, the tarnished gold of chains that had been etched by the sea's might and mystery over countless ages, always altered but never impaired by limitless tides, and surviving the wrath of untold tempests …

Tempests.

From a title of a piece masterfully steeped in magic and sorcery, to the current riddle of gruesome importance.

To my family, to me, to how many others.

And Abby – she, too, has seen the spectre of this thing.

For as all were leaving, her hand had gone over his arm – and held him back. He had stayed on, to hear her describe in detail the very same volume seen in vision one dark day.

That gentle tale, of the Wizard with his magic Book – *The Tempest*, with its curious absence of any connection, any solid link to any of the legends and stories that the Bard had freely stolen and exploited – now it loomed over him, like a beacon, both signpost and warning.

Did he know?

Did he see the source of the story himself and subvert the truth into fantasy?

If so, did he ever imagine that what he figured so well in verse could possibly resurface? A Book of Power. An actual Wizard – brother against brother.

Whose brother?

Do I not now have nearly a brother?

Who is Tam's father?

He had come to a stop.

The moon's glow clung to him, as cool as the breath of the approaching autumn, with its attendant mists and shadowed moods.

It came to him suddenly, a sense of longing, of upheaval, as if there were no ground beneath his boots. He had traveled so far, in time and space, since that night when it all began, when a flame-haired beauty had opened to him new worlds of savage wonder, of fearful darkness and brilliant light, of terror and new-found sovereignty.

It was through her that I passed into this brave, new world – from what I was – to what I am.

And still I walk forward – hungry for a place different from one here, one far distant, where summer reigns, where the golden aura of rich warmth teases the senses, and invites the sensibilities to wax fruitful.

I seek an island in this void around me that I have made myself, peopled too much, perhaps with monsters – an Island – Prospero's Island – where like him, resides the courage I lack now – and where the freedom he sought awaits me.

I need a miracle.

He walked on, crossing street after street, his pace beat for beat with his heart, then stumbled, brought to a halt by a cracked pavement.

He looked down.

Once again came the shock of *'now'*; horror had come full circle.

Directly in his path was a broad, bright mark.

It was a declaration of ongoing war, recent, limned in blood that glistened fresh and black in the moon's stern light – an enormous covenant straight from a world of nightmare.

The track of the Cat.

Racing now, the Mage followed the spoor of the deadly creature until the hair lifted along his neck.

I know where he's gone.

Breathless, concealed in the shadows of a lofty pine, he stood finally before the Fitzalan home.

The signs led up the drive, lost to sight along the side of the house.

The back. If that Thing has gotten in …

He studied the building and exhaled a curse.

Dark again? How in Hell can the house be dark again?

It was arguably the worst possible time for the place to be so encumbered; he cursed the modern age, which had rendered this place too dark, too often in defiance of its automatic light settings.

He knelt, sickened by the acrid scent of blood in his face – crouching over the brick path that curled to the rear of the house. The old pavers there ranged far, deep into the gardens where now unkempt verdure ruled. Eyes on foliage that might well figure as his last resting place, Cass followed the track.

Fitzalan's home was grand in scale, his gardens a masterpiece, denser and considerably more remarkable than those at the Hythe residence.

This is what comes from perfect concepts and execution – both of the Elizabethan period.

A wonder, with all its history and significance intact – and now, a death-trap.

Since his return, the Mage had ventured into the gardens often – but never at night.

Iain's gardens shared their links to the past with another great house.

For within the labyrinthine walks, Fitzalan had also reared up a knot garden, at whose centre, he had erected a thing curious beyond measure.

Why in the world would he have left it here, here in deep shade, out of reach of all reasonable use – the sundial?

It was a compelling little mystery, one that might forever remain so, for Cass wished now he had had the chance to ask the answer of such an astonishing man, in person. But Iain was gone, long dead in either past one chose to consider, and his gardens were overgrown – and infinitely dangerous.

As was his house – a cenotaph in every way.

Both gone; father and daughter.

91

Too many memories, far too many …

With an effort, the Sorcerer scanned again the trees, and finally, the many heavy oak doors, firmly shut against the shadows of lost time, the memory of lost lives.

Not quite shut.

There. The one into the south face – that one from the knot garden into the house – that is ajar.

As silent as the Cat, Cass drew near, and there, at the stone entryway with its surface carpeted by the dry scattered leaves of a tumultuous summer – he found the mark of his quarry.

Ebony in moonlight was the blood on the step; pale was the face of the Mage as he accepted the dark invitation and stepped forward.

It's been some time since Cat and I held contest.

He'll find I've changed.

As he froze in the doorway, listening intently, light glittered off his wand, and the honed dagger he clutched in his hands – and he entered the rear kitchen hall, and into a dark house.

Spectral in vacancy, not a single suggestion of anything preternatural met him now. He navigated the vast rustic kitchen; reaching the hall, he stopped again, so still that he might have been carved in stone.

It came.

From the study – the slightest of sounds, nearly indistinguishable at this moment from the fitful grumbling of a very old house.

Yet it sufficed; from nothing, a faint blue mist rose over the wand's tip — and another sound, infinitely more furtive recurred.

Alarm increased exponentially in the Mage's mind, for here, within the house, there was yet no sign of the Cat either in spoor or spirit. Caspian Hythe readied his weapons.

All right, then – come.

I hunger for thee … Tam.

As if in infernal retort to his challenge – in the far doorway of the study, a figure appeared.

Darker than the shadows it stood, etched in the silver of heaven's emissary of mystery, of all things veiled and enigmatic. And Cass tensed for, now, the hidden one glided closer – and stepped full into the moonlight.

A voice, soft and unmistakable rang – and the Sorcerer cried out as, with her red hair gleaming like purest gold – Ava Fitzalan, the Knight, strode forward into the room.

CHAPTER 10

TÊTE-Á-TÊTE

Silently, Quist sipped the hot beverage.

One of the library doors to the Hythe gardens remained ajar; he was grateful for the breeze, it was just cool enough to lift curls of steam off his cup. Those curls danced in fantastic shapes; increasingly and vaguely alarmed with no apparent basis, the scholar dimly heard Abby's voice. Her chatter was as ephemeral as the clouds over his chocolate until, abashed, she, too, slipped into silence.

Quist regarded the room; familiar yet not; for the world had changed somehow yet once more, and once again, it seemed for the worse.

"Well, my dear, about a century ago, you certainly said a mouthful."

Abby sighed; she tipped her head back against the couch and returned his regard. Monty's eyes twinkled beneath those famed brows, but his look was sharp and appraising. Abby was nowhere near tears; it came to her guest that he had never seen her cry, not openly.

Not even when Randolph passed.
I thought then she was made of sterner stuff.

But never, not until this very minute, did I see the true strength – the power of this lady.

He recalled them all at that breathless moment just hours before when his hostess had revealed herself; himself speechless, Percy with an extraordinary and unfathomable look as he exchanged a glance with Abby – and Cass, whose expression went from bafflement to resignation.

Closed he became; like shutters drawn, like a cloak drawn tight.

Caspian Hythe.

The meeting had ended. The scholar had been halfway home when he had pulled his car to the kerb.

Call it premonition; in this case, it was one more instance of 'thought made actual' – a *voice* – and the need to return to the Hythe house had become imperative.

For a long moment; he had stood in the street, regarding the house. Then he had rung the bell. No surprise to him to see the lights still on – no surprise on Abby's face when she had met him at the door.

What is it about this family?

Now I hear voices all the time, or is it rather I hear them when I am supposed to?

The 'thought' made actual in Fitzalan's library months before; Cass had been certain that that had been the Sylph, there in the room with me.

Imagine it – a life imbued, surrounded by the activity of such entities. And Abby has been smack in the middle of this, from the beginning.

Now, he saw her with new eyes, how her steadfastness, her very steadiness, had held fast the doors against a very real darkness, in so many ways.

All the while holding close a very dark secret – her link to this young assassin – and his new pet, that still amplifying germ and agent of the Black Queen.

I am nonplussed; I am amazed. Could it get any worse?

"You're staring, Monty."

Her voice, low, chiding, always ironical brought him back. She had picked up the Orb; the lovely mystery perched in her palm like a small happy puppy, he thought. He studied her as she poured again, the lady he thought he knew so well, and all that came to mind were those deceptively innocent and charming lines from Lewis Carroll …

'How doth the little crocodile improve his shining tail … how cheerfully he seems to grin, how neatly spreads his claws – and welcomes little fishes in – with gently smiling jaws!'

Whose jaws, Abby?

"Forgive me, Abby. But it seems we're not quite done yet, with any of it, are we?"

Frozen mid-pour, she put down Orb and carafe.

"I am thinking on Cass."

Cass; a former nephew, a current orphan, now truly alone in the world; or was he?

"Abby, won't you open your mind to me – if not your heart? He took the ring with him, didn't he?"

She stared.

"How did you guess?"

"I felt it somehow, from the room, from your voice. It troubles you."

"Yes; and no. The coming of the ring was foretold – oh, not as a 'ring of power' like in the fairy stories. But as something that confers great strength, or effects great destiny. No, it's a little thing to anyone but Cass, or someone like him – to them it speaks of everything – to the future, it *spells out* a lot of what that future will be. And in his hands, on his hand – it *spells power*. And Monty, the pivotal word is *'spells'*.

She rose; from the desk, she brought her own slender wand – and she laid it beside the Eye of the First Gryphon.

"Monty, I can't explain it all, not in one sentence or in one sitting. I can say that the Star Taker, the pieces of that thing when all assembled, can show the way to the Book – *and much more*. But it still lacks a vital Key – to open the Book or to close it – *as we must*. That Key is neither clear, nor manifest."

He said nothing.

"You are thinking."

"No, Abby, I am computing the odds."

She laughed; the sound was startling, all the more so due to the hour and the circumstance.

"Dear Heaven, do we have any chance in Hell of surviving this?" he cried.

"Yes. Perhaps one ... in Hell."

To his surprise, she took his hand and abruptly raised it to her lips. Montgomery Quist, scholar, adventurer, and collector squeezed hers. The rich strength in her laughter, the hubris, or perhaps the plain and simple humanity, with all its much bewailed frailty – and its dull but undeniable fortitude reassured him somehow.

Like the cry, thrilling and keen – of a hawk, high overhead, floating somehow in the air, with its wings wide and defiant – against a brutal, callous tempest.

Here we sit, two old friends in a dark old library, with the moon ready to set and a cold, uncertain wind at our backs – on the edge of possible and very imminent doom.

"Monty, if I could be only half way certain of any future – near or otherwise, I'd be the first one to offer you odds."

Now he gazed down at the relic she held again, still amazed at the artistry that could yield a surface so ancient, so seamless, so pure. And he recalled that Iain Fitzalan and a magical predecessor had both held this thing, held it safe, until it had passed back and forth through time.

Until now.

Abby held out the Orb; after a moment's hesitation, the scholar took it into his hand.

He looked into the perfect sphere of crystal. The sound of the fire in its grate softened finally into a low and intimate discourse held between flame and flue. The room seemed to darken, slipping free of the fire's grip.

He looked deeper.

"Wait. What's that, there in the haze in the Orb?"

Soft and sweet as a dear memory, for a second the sigh of the sea came to him, muted, alluring, just as it had come at the Pool.

Something changed; without warning, there came voices from deep within the Orb and by turns warm then cold, the relic suddenly took on *life* – and *stirred* in his hand.

A scene, dim then increasingly clear unfolded, curling up from within the milky depths. Then it came – the images and words were darkened with age and mystery, but it was surely the map he had found long ago, or one devilishly akin – and ancient and corrupt, a Latin phrase came startlingly clear to his view.

'Locus.

Genius Loci … 'The Place …The Spirit of the Place.'

"The Place – wait, I know what that means, I know where that is," he cried.

100

Fewer than a handful of his colleagues might have made the same declaration.

Fleeing from revelation, the image faded, to be replaced by one far more sinister.

In his mind's eye, he stood within a grotto.

Light flickered down from the cloistered ceiling of sea-ravaged rock high above.

From the walls about him, water dripped, in incessant chorus to the rise and fall of tides, and the scent of fresh ocean mingled with the green perfumes of dulse and spume.

In the very centre of the grotto was a well.

Sea tangle crunched under his feet as he stepped forward to peer downward where shallow water, held captive within the deep well of the grotto, sparkled in constant shifting ripples.

And there – below the water's surface, on the ledge directly below the bore's salt encrusted lip – came the flash of gold, where an object adorned with clasps, golden and verdigris, was rising into reach, moment by moment freed from the constant cyclic clutch and cloak of the sea.

Under his eyes, the sinking waters made a last caress over the thing, hissing across the tarnished golden chains that yet confined the locks.

He stretched downward, in a few breaths more the thing would be within his reach.

And as he bent to the dripping black stones, a sound ventured out, warring with the rhythmic song of the waves – it was harsh, bestial – and he gazed across the well to the opposite side of the grotto where a dark and high cavern gaped from within the stony wall itself.

And from the shadows within, two eyes flashed out. And they were red, demonic, flaming with lust and greed and fury, and fixed upon him.

Red eyes – like that dreadful Cat, like those of the damned Rabbit 'Below'…

In terror, he cried out; falling backward, his hand raked across the sharp, shell-encrusted stone of the well's lip. Searing pain shot upward from his hand. Blood dripped down, the stream of blood fell and caught on the object below – and chaos erupted.

He felt as well as heard the chains splitting, the grinding of metal shearing from itself – and the terrible roar of voices that cried aloud in anger, in joy, in freedom and bloodlust.

And with that cacophony of exultant horror, darkness surged and came alive, reaching up, seeking hungrily from the object and the well itself – and dark clawed hands, of no colour and of every hue imaginable lunged for his throat.

Montgomery Quist came to his senses on the floor beside the couch. Abigail Fitzalan was beside him; he was crying, his mind overthrown by the terror, by the spectacle that no man should see and remain sane.

The Orb was beside him as well and when the shaken man reached for the thing that had opened time and space once again, he saw to his dismay that his hand was torn and still bleeding.

Quist had seen and experienced much since the day Abigail's then nephew had first come to his study. But this was too much – the simple sight of the blood on his hand was beyond his capacity. For a full minute, he raved, nearly succumbing to it, to the implication, to the madness he had seen.

"*Was I there?* Was I truly there? Yet it was day, not night as it is now," came his choked words.

But here was a man of strength and ultimate reason. Shaking off the clutch of horror, he rose nearly unaided to his feet, then sat again on the sofa.

Abby got brandy into him, got his wounds tended and then her arms went round him.

"I saw it too – oh, my dear Monty, forgive me," she murmured.

He held the Orb; it was clear and cool and quite still in his hand.

As though you are waiting for something; for me to take up the gauntlet, perhaps?

I shall.

But I know you, now, you little trap for the souls of men and others.

You little trinket of the Wise; you have shown me that I am in deep waters, indeed.

But I say to you – I have been in them before.

He put the thing down, with a sudden wave of new purpose, new determination.

His eyes went round the room, a room whose shadows seemed deeper, darker, more expectant than shadows had any right to be. In the grate, the fire was weak but determined; as was Quist himself.

"No. *I won't forgive you.* Not unless you start talking – right now."

CHAPTER II

ADIT/EXIT

"My Sorcerer."

For a full ten seconds, Caspian Hythe stood as one shot, with his tongue hewed to the roof of his mouth.

"Cass."

He stared down at his weapons, the dagger bright in one shaking hand – his wand in the other.

Then, both slid ignominiously onto the floor. How he crossed the room he would never remember; all that stayed with him was the softness of her cheek against his hand as he raised her face to his, all that mattered was the look in her eyes – that gaze so much older, somehow more wary, nay – more fierce, than he had ever witnessed *'Below'*.

Petal soft was his touch across the full lips; light as breath his fingertips wiping the tears from the face of the lost one. With another cry, his arms went round her, both lost to all for a precious moment, until the terrible urgency of his intent in this house forced him to his senses.

She looked up into his face.

"I don't know where to begin," he said.

"Hasn't that been our problem since the beginning?"

He kissed her again, deeply.

"Amongst others," came his whisper – then his gaze darkened, his eyes became stormy.

"You can't be here. The Cat has risen somehow – he's here, and he's already killed."

The Knight's expression did not change; not a mote of concern crossed the fair features, not a look askance came into the beautiful eyes and the Mage glared at her.

"You know this! *How do you know this?*" he demanded.

"I *do know* – this and a great many other things, now, Cass. I also know *he can't enter here.*"

Speechless he turned away.

There was the hall to Iain's famed library, there the stairwell, all familiar, all exquisite in shadow and light yet somehow all inviolable. He returned to her, brimming with the questions that had plagued him these many months and more.

"I left you *'Below'*. I tried to open the Gate, to bring you through. But I failed, Ava, I failed."

Her eyes became brilliant; positively ferocious was the look she cast on the Mage.

"Caspian Hythe – *you did not fail*. Not then, not now. But believe me, the Cat has risen *because* all of the pieces necessary are now in place, and something hideous advances on us, even as I speak. It's going to be a question of life or death for not just you and me, but for all of us."

Never had the Knight spoken thus, so resolutely, so imperatively. He pulled back and, taking the ring from his pocket, he held it out to her on his palm.

"Is this one of the pieces?"

He heard her sharp intake of breath; Ava's eyes widened. Fear, awe, resignation and hope – all blazed there at the sight of the ancient relic, and her words were low and harsh.

"No. Don't let me touch it, for yours alone is the voice it needs to hear. You know what that is now, don't you, Cass?"

"It's the ring I saw in my vision *'Below'*; this was on my finger the first time I spoke with Him."

"It is yours, a mark of what you were, a presage of what you may be – and the final proof that all that passed before, bringing you and I to this point …"

Her voice failed; there was no need for more.

"It's bad this time. Again. And again, the time is suddenly now."

He looked down on the little gold thing – and slowly, as if he were carefully turning a page in a mighty book – slowly, his fist closed over the ring's cool surface.

The room in which they stood vanished.

Gasping for breath, with every movement an agony, the Mage stood now alone in a vaulting cavern, vast and dark. Pale light streamed down to reveal wet, black walls laden with brine, cast and chiseled by the work of a thousand young seas and storms. And the stony cavern trembled; the wet rocks shook beneath his feet.

Weary and faint, in sorrow, in loss – he heard the distant chant of the pounding sea; that call came sweet and compelling, echoing from far away.

Undine.

Then *light* surged around him, dim at first, then welling brightly, and he saw below him the deep chasm, hewn from the living rock, where water still roiled and churned.

And as he stood on the narrow, stony path adjoined with the weeds of the deeps, he saw that he himself was wounded, and bleeding. The dark waters surged, rising up angrily, *hungrily* – and then fell – and with a deep shudder the earth, ravaged, violated, cried out, in fear and torment.

For below him now, lying exposed to the frail air of an unready world, was something bound in gold, with its hasps limned, shackled and girt in gold, as ancient as it was horrible.

The Drownéd Book.

For with new-found vision, the Sorcerer *saw* – that the gold was a lure to the unwary, bait for the unwise – that the image of the Book was only that,

108

that its form was illusory – that the true nature of the thing was savage, corrupt and altogether uncontrollable.

And beside the thing bound in gold came two more flashes, equally bright.

On the sea-washed ledge right beside the Book, not one but two pieces of the astrolabe, the Star Taker, lay waiting, as water lapped their edges – in expectation. And to his eyes – darkness began to form as the Book fought against its bonds – *fought to open.*

It is a Gateway into dark 'space', where ancient knowledge, abased by the minds and hearts of faithless men walks hand in hand in tainted covenant – one bound in blood and misery – with the darkest forces in this and every world.

It is not a Book – it is a snare, a net of deception and evil, and the darkness I see is the maelstrom of destruction – a portal.

Not to good, but to inestimable evil.

And he stood there, bleeding in an agony of despair, of need – and the voices within the Book's pages rose up, calling to him in words of praise and promise – as his blood began to drip down, into the waters …

And the Sorcerer stood on the brink – and the world beyond the sunken chamber held its breath as he moved the ring from fist – to finger – and the voices and spirit of what humankind ignorantly labels as Hell started up, tasting imminent triumph, basking

in the terrible exultation in the Mage's burning eyes
…

"My Sorcerer."

With a start, the vision sheared away from his sight, and Caspian Hythe was again in Fitzalan's home, standing beside the mistress of that place, and as he looked at her anew, he saw that not only had *he* changed utterly with her loss – but *she* had changed as well.

"Do you trust me, Cass?"

Awful the look in her brilliant eyes, awful was that question, the very same he had asked of her *'Below'* when he had been tempted to use his untried power, to use a word of *Command*, to bend the Knight to his will.

To my desire.

And I need her – I desire her as never before.

He hesitated; here was an unknown potency. It radiated from the Knight, even as it had from him, that night when he had so nearly subverted his sovereignty – and had been tempted to do again, just now.

Tests – then, and now.

Not knowing who or what stood beside him now, he spoke.

"I do."

"Then come."

One look round the room, for it might be the last – then the Mage recovered his weapons, and they left.

Like the afterthought of a pistol shot – such was the hushed click of the front door as it closed behind the two.

Silence once more filled the Fitzalan house; moonlight governed the vacant rooms in gentle splendour as, one by one, the stars in the mute heavens made imperceptible yet irrevocable tracks – forward.

Opal light fled softly across the floors; shadow reclaimed its office – as the door to the garden opened again.

Along the very path where the Mage's steps had made their marks, now came different footfalls.

Firm they were; bold yet stealthy were the steps of the one who followed in the wake of the Sorcerer. All sound ceased as the interloper stopped, standing very nearly where the Mage and the Knight had made their conference.

Bathed in the fast abating light, Tam stood motionless.

He surveyed the hall, the rooms adjoining.

His gaze went to the door, where his eyes sought to read the very substance of those who had passed through moments before, as if he would gauge the scope of their designs, united once more in passion – in power.

He did not stand there alone.

As silent as an apparition, it came from behind, a Thing of null being, of *unexistence*, of no worlds and all spaces – pure chaos reveling in the trappings of incarnate Evil – and the purr of the Cat filled the room with the lust and pleasure of a demon finding infernal voice.

"Shall we follow," the Cat wondered.

"No. Not yet. First, nearer to the prize."

The Cat's eyes glowed feverishly.

"Then?"

"Yes, then. Then – we can both play."

The damned creature followed with delight as Tam made his way into Iain's library. There, Abby's prodigal son made quick and determined search. Book after book, tome by tome, Tam's fingers flew across page after page. And in much less than an hour, he turned from his labour.

In his hand was a slip of ancient paper.

It was only a fragment; Tam had hoped for much more. But the text in the parchment was nearly intact – and the diagram precisely what he had needed.

And the whole was in the hand of Iain Fitzalan.

Tam's gaze was triumphant, and the Cat, curled contentedly in colossal menace rose to its feet.

"Now?"

"Yes, now."

The two left as they had come, in stealth. There was little sign of their incursion; when the rear door closed gently after them, the house once more fell to stillness.

Stealth is not the same as secrecy; silence may not be the stillness of vacancy.

Slowly, the quiet changed; silence took on a strangely animated accent, as though the timbers themselves had roused into an animation utterly unseen but fiercely palpable.

The moon took her long awaited rest.

And when the library succumbed finally under the full sway of deep night, with His gaze fixed firmly on the shelves that Tam had searched – the Master appeared fully and strode across that room.

He appraised the scattered lore and veritable quintessence of the owner – and His hand rose slowly. Sheer light shone about the spread digits – and the gold ring on His finger blazed briefly.

Aglow in shimmering sapphire, the books and catalogs rustled softly in their places until one, burning more ardently – pulled free from its dusty slot. The Master took the book – it opened in his hands.

> *What is not seen is often the determinant factor.*
> *For even a fool can see what lies in plain sight.*
> *The wise fool seeks what is missing.*

And the One who had drawn in Caspian Hythe through the medium of Ava Fitzalan, into a new and perilous existence *called*, and revealed the missing page as it surged out of the book, into sharp life in the restive air.

Like a waiting servant, there in the air it hung.

There was the map to the Place of Need, there clearly, the urn, the points in the stones.

There was the one stone within whose dark recesses – one of the Signs lay – all appeared before the Master.

He nodded. The tome returned to its place and the Great One pondered.

All is as was beheld.

The scholar has this same, and the faithful follow.

Now it truly does begin – perhaps to the death.

I cannot retreat – may They be merciful, for now – all my plans are fit …

As the last of the light left the room, the One standing now in complete darkness turned, and departed.

CHAPTER 12

YOUNG MAN'S FANCY

In the fireplace, a log fell and a spray of sparks danced up into the flue; it brought a hard stare from the lady, and from the gentleman on the sofa.

Abby took up the Orb and rose to her feet. She stopped at the half open door. For many moments she stood there in the doorway, hesitating between the illusory refuge of the room where her friend now demanded answers – and the real world, the brutal one outside the Hythe house, where strange ungovernable roads, and stranger travelers awaited.

"It is indeed a journey, a trial – not quite done yet."

She had spoken from the doorway, as though she were addressing someone hidden in the shadowy gardens, and Quist strained to make out her words.

"Lovers of truth, aren't they – all your family, Monty?"

It was a queer question, at a time like this.

"Why, yes, we are all dusty academics, if you will – all lovers of things past."

She turned to him.

"Of a *good mystery*, you mean. For what else is history but a handful of legends that, through pain

115

and cleverness, we deliver into prominence and then baptise into fact. No surprise then; so it is – as they are, so are you."

He came to full attention.

"Why, I suppose that is so."

"Things, Monty, run in families, don't they."

He studied her closely now, with the most perfect sensation of foreboding – for she held a monstrous, monstrous thing in her hand as he might have held a teacup.

"You are saying the 'Force' is strong in your family? Ridiculous phrase…"

"But quite apt, Monty. Come you didn't raise a brow when I observed how clever you are in archaeology, when so many of your family – your line – are precisely that."

"No; I see the analogy."

"So it was that once upon a time, there was a remarkable family.

And there in the midst of all these wonderful minds, was a very lonely, and I might say – very foolish young woman. A girl, really; oh, she was as bright as her brother, but not nearly so witty – more shy. And sadly, more in need of *proving* something – to herself – and to all the rest of them, who thought of her in the kindest terms – but in a way that made her feel – *insubstantial*.

Hungry for knowledge, for *power* – she taught herself what seemed natural, becoming ever more proficient in things that most girls never would think of when the word 'adept' was used.

And one day – quite a golden afternoon it was – her brother, well – he disappeared for some time.

It wasn't really very long, just enough to frighten all the rest. And when he re-appeared many hours later – he *seemed* – he *was* quite different. Pale, disquieted and determinedly silent about what he had been doing in the time he had been absent – and where precisely he had been.

Older, more thoughtful; it was no surprise to his sister at least when he began to seek out books – the oldest, the strangest ones he could find. And what he found grew into a collection, a library, the likes of which few have seen.

And he collected other things, as well.

He sought out new friends, some of whom are more than familiar to you now. He became obsessed with protecting his family – and specifically that one girl – now so nearly a woman.

It wasn't quite enough.

For one day, when most of the family were absent – a man appeared. At least that is what he appeared to be. He was handsome and charming; he radiated a strength, a power both stirring – and irresistible. He chose a time when that brother was away, searching, hunting … for what seemed the impossible – and that man found a way to meet, more than once, that lonely, very hungry young woman .."

Quist drew back.

Cold in his nerveless hand and almost on its own, his cup slid free. It tumbled slowly, end over end to shatter on the floor.

Neither the woman or the man spoke. And the scholar regarded the lady across from him with dread. She again fixed wide and beautiful eyes on him, and looked deeply into his own.

The fire left off crackling in its grate; instead, it shrank down, as the man who loved a good mystery realised something extraordinary – that he was suddenly afraid of Abby. He wondered why what he felt now was so akin to what he had felt some time ago – when he had found a skeleton in a sarcophagus within a not quite lifeless church.

It is the same; that of the dead trying to rise – to speak – that of a not so harmless past reaching for us – coming alive again.

And still the fire seemed to die, fleeing from the shadows that all of a sudden were everywhere and completely independent of the imminent lack of a fire in the grate. Light dwindled; with it went that transient sense of any certainty, any sense of comfort – all of it curled within the scholar and shrank into a cold mass somewhere near his stomach.

The sense of some grim horror approaching was stifling; with an effort he got the words out in a whisper.

"Abby. Tell me now. Where are the other pieces of that damned astrolabe – what exactly is it that opens the Book – *and who is Tam's father?*"

She went pale; beside the couch, she looked down on him with a look of grim misery – and then her hand went to her brow in desperation.

Then he heard her cry out – and her eyes were on the library door across from them.

"The breeze, Monty. What has happened to the breeze?"

For the wind had died.

Yet purposefully did the library door move now of its own accord – and a dreadful sound, soft and furtive came from the shadows, and the Professor cried out, even as the moment became the last.

"What is that?"

CHAPTER 13

LADY AND TIGER

One can't have everything … or can one?

What was more to the point is that most often, the price of having everything is losing everything that one already has – already cherishes. This of course, was immaterial to the young lady sitting in the dark in the bed.

When she had gone away to university, Pen had never given up this set of tiny rooms close to Percy's training studio. Now they proved a haven, for the swordsman's nearest kin needed the solitude of her own thoughts.

It's bad when all you can do is sit in bed holding your knees.

Late; almost nothing left of the night, and she swiveled to the edge of the bed.

A sliver of light on her face; the look there was uncharacteristically troubled, and she struggled with her bed linen.

I am not an unhappy person.

I am not easy to fool – to beguile.

But what I've seen tonight has given me pause; as it should, to any sane person, any scientist.

She considered herself a scientist; history, the complexity of languages, English and worldwide – these were not trifles in thought or philosophy.

It's not rocket science, often it's more complex, much harder – and less respected.

So much less … significant.

It had been a momentous journey thus far; from a pleasant visit to a favourite uncle – to the edge of a discovery of world –stopping proportions.

At least in her world.

Yet a slight but critical demarcation, an extraordinary line lay in her way – her world now overlapped the world of an individual of such mystery – for the Hythe man was undecipherable.

Not just to me – to anyone in this modern age.

There are no sorcerers – there should not be wizards.

At least none that we can prove – and a Book of Power? How much more unreasonable, how much more impossible.

After all, this isn't the next summer block buster – it is real life.

Or is it? The question truly is – what is real life?

What we see, what we say we know – what actually exists just outside that? What goes merrily on in the dark outside the light we get from instant news, daily tweets – the meaningless chatter of an enlightened, modern age?

And did I just meet – and see more deeply – one of those denizens of the world 'outside' – just hours ago.

There are 'lost years' in the life of that famed playwright.

And we know he spent time in the south of England – for there he had a patron – on a rocky coast where the land meets the sea – an estuary of visual islands …

And Prospero was born in his mind, the Wizard with his magic Cloak – his magic Book.

And the astrolabe is real – that I could touch, I could hold it in my hand – and Caspian Hythe is just as inexplicable now, after much clear and careful analysis, away from the shadow play of a room with gold trinkets and such – as he was minutes ago…

How does he do it? How does he appear to do it?

She went to the window.

She saw suddenly how it was; how we bumble along, overly impressed with ourselves, immersed in the minutiae of our lives. When we do raise our eyes we do not see the fires of the stars; we see instead the smog, the weather that will hasten or hinder our commutes next morning.

Those I met tonight, when they look up – they see galaxies. They are all deep – deep in things much greater than themselves.

And I am suddenly hungry – for what they know, what they've done – hungry, for knowledge – for power.

And this other one – what of this enemy?

Clearly an unstable fellow – or is he just being really clever – really manipulative?

He wants to kill Abby, it seems – or does he?

Isn't it more a matter of creating a lure, an impetus – her death might be just the threat, the push to get the rest of them moving – moving where? If I wished to force the game to hasten – this is how I'd do it.

But what is the endgame – the goal.

We have only one piece of that thing – where are the others – and once they're united – what then?

If I could get my hands on the rest – if I could be certain the Book is real – what could I not do? It's better than a lottery, that is just money.

This is the chance to work enormous good, to cure the world. The power of good …

But Cass – still there, still the great unknown.

She went over the events of the night again. At first, she had watched in frank disbelief as words had formed where words could not be seen; it had not been a parlour trick. Her doubt had evaporated.

It was more than a trick of the light; the very atmosphere of the room changed.

No trick; I am immune to such sophistry. Something inexplicable was happening in that room – with just his hand – and Cass was the source.

The look in the Mage's eyes came to her with sudden clarity.

Those eyes were nearly grey. But as he had worked this thing they grew stormy, as were the steel, dark waves of the seas as they tower in open ocean, when storm clouds scudded overhead – when the tempest came.

Cass – the unknown quantity.

What if he isn't what he seems to be. What if there's more – if he has his own agenda.

Does the average Sorcerer still have an Achilles heel – and how does one take advantage of it?

He is after all – just a man – with all a man's frailties – all a man's desires.

Fascinated – compelled somehow – I must act.

I was ready to give it up – academia.

There's easier ways to feed the cat. Is this evening a sign – that I should stay on? Now I sound like them – all stewing in magic, in signs.

But I can't deny what I saw.

It is so hard to know what to do. What am I to do? How can I join in this undertaking – it's what's been missing – what I see now I've been longing for all my life.

The chance of a lifetime and this man, this Caspian Hythe will be a part of it.

I am strong; I am clever – I don't need anything more.

What I need is a miracle.

Drowsy, disordered, she left the window and returned to the bed. The pillow needed punching; it didn't pan out as usual. Still no calm; no sleep.

For suddenly, this life of hers, this stream of regulated, fairly successful minutiae had suffered a sea change. No longer enough, that old life slipped away from her like sinking water in a deep well whose walls had been breached – to reveal something wonderful.

Something rich and strange – wonderful beyond words – something golden – a golden opportunity – the chance of a lifetime.

And so it is, Lady.

Breathless, eyes wide – she started up at the voice that seemed not like that of conscience, of guidance that a quick intellect and solid temperament was used to hearing in the mind.

This sounded all too real.

It is – Come.

Faltering, she hesitated on the point of a knife, the sense that this might be the first clear signpost of madness, of too much stress, too much astonishment.

But sweet, inviting, somewhere between male and female, and far too low to easily determine either source or identity – again came words, chiding but generous.

It is not hard at all.

Not really; it is easy.

Come.

"All right, damn it – I'm coming."

One should never talk back to the imaginary voice.

Yet, she had. And she had flung back the covers, ready to confront demons, whether personal or otherwise.

Back to the window, where she yanked away curtains, threw the casement fully open.

To the night, in all its fleeting glory.

The shadows up and down the old street were darker than she had ever seen before and it was hard to make out anything – much less the one with the imaginary voice.

So still; a silence constraining and unnatural met the young woman at the window. The moon was setting; stars blazed out, comfortingly – invitingly – and the scientist searched the heavens for a glimpse of just one galaxy.

Tonight, the galaxy would be found in the street.

Lady.

Again; dulcet yet commanding tones drew her startled stare downward.

There in the street, shadows from the trees, from the clouds, all conspired to cast a mosaic of light and dark across the way.

From the darkest of these, a figure stepped.

Tall, the features still cloaked in darkness, yet she could see the face was turned up – to hers – and even in the gloom came the gleam of eyes.

It is not hard at all, to know what to do.

Before she could speak, the figure stepped away, back into the dark beneath the boughs.

In pursuit, she took the narrow stairs two at a time and flung open the front door. Night again met her full in the face, one of the darkest she had seen.

The stones of the porch were icy under her bare feet; she stood shivering with the cold, with the sheer thrill of emotion that the entirely unforeseen always brings.

Cloud covered the moon's pale sliver – yet light shone – from below her – from her feet.

There on the pavers below her, in the path leading to the street – was a box.

She knelt to it; it was neither large nor overly long, with burnished wood, and finished with polished brass at ends and front.

With a last look into the now voiceless night, she picked it up.

Inside, Pen sat upon the stairs wondering, perhaps as Pandora wished she had – more deeply. Then as Pandora had – Pen opened the box.

She looked long, then slowly closed the little casket. Still staring at it, she left it on the stair.

In a moment, she returned to her place – and retrieved the contents.

She could not resist; she was an adept of a fine swordsman, a warrior in a long line of warriors.

The niece of the swordsman sat in the dark of the stairwell and looked down on beauty, on elegance sublimely wrought in silver and gold and the brightest of honed steel.

She gazed down on a thing created with one purpose only in mind – to kill.

On a dagger.

CHAPTER 14

TURNING POINTS

"But it truly is the chance of a lifetime."

"No doubt, Pen. But whose lifetime? And at what cost?"

The talk had been some time ago.

The mood of the swordsman had passed through grim, limped across indecision, and landed squarely on despair.

In one of the darkest moments of his existence, Percy Onslow now stood alone in his studio.

The same moon that had lent so much clarity, such revelation to the Sorcerer, his adversary and the Master painted the features of the sword master in only the faintest, most subdued palette. Bleak seemed all that night to him; terrible, for his fears had been realised.

For Abby had spoken; her words had struck the room to silence. He had felt no such amazement, no such awe, and for reasons his companions, his dearest friends would have found unaccountable – reprehensible.

Appalling. Unforgiveable. But necessary.

Only Cass; he alone would have marked my reticence. He alone, for he alone of us dwells now not only in our world – physical, casual and superficial – but also in the realms of spirituality, of metaphysical sensibility that we, up until quite recently could not have encountered, or even imagined.

As for the Mage, perhaps not even he, alone.…

Percy had not told Pen; his niece remained oblivious – and now he was grateful for that reticence

Not even she knows the extent of my involvement, my folly.

He glanced over – there, since the day the Mage had nearly killed him – rested the sword of Fitzalan.

The weapons on his walls that gave a profound new meaning to the verb 'display' glowed richly in the sky's fading light. Here he had been happy, productive – and close. Here he had kept an existence unquestioned by those he had instructed, those with whom he had shared blessed intimacy – of care – of a simple, common humanity that was increasingly in sharp contrast to what had come tonight – and would come tomorrow.

It has been a life of comparative safety, as in the difference between holding a blade, and a finely honed one.

For the secret stayed with Abby – and with me.

That time was past.

With her announcement, with the recovery of the ring, with the sudden and terrifying return of that one piece of the Taker – the signs could not be clearer.

They will never be clearer again.

Thus, he had waited, waited and watched, as instructed – as entreated, and by more than one of the players in this next most terrible chapter of the game, and now …

It has come.

The day I dreaded, that many dreaded, the night that is only a hint of the darker, more impenetrable nights that are to come – if we falter, if we read the signs amiss – if we cannot unite to drive It back.

And it is just as before, a little matter of those affairs 'Below', and the legacy of Iain Fitzalan.

Abby.

Her son.

And the father of that child.

And in my lifetime – I so wished it would not have been in my lifetime – I so wish Pen had not come down from Oxford.

Damn his genius, damn his arrogance.

He revealed almost nothing of the truth; it was still too much by far.

That quaint story of the island bound Wizard and his Book – how deftly had its author veiled it all, bent the story to conceal the thing – the place – the threat.

And if Iain was correct – and blast it, when wasn't he – that is not the only thing we must fear.

Even if it meant that Ava could never again stand with them, suddenly he felt a great longing to speak with that man – Fitzalan – to hear again that deep voice, that intoxicating laughter. Once more to share the scope of his vision, as he worked the countless little miracles that had so nearly ensured his sister, her erstwhile nephew, and his own daughter – would be given the best of chances.

To survive, to live, to bring into this close and extraordinary fold, one of the most remarkable of young men.

For strange and often imponderable is Caspian Hythe – as is the daughter of Iain Fitzalan herself.

And now all my intents have shifted again.

For just moments ago, it seemed, as he had lingered in the studio in the dark – his door had opened. And on the threshold, there was One, imagined if not known – and amazed at the words he heard but compliant, Onslow accepted.

And once more agreed that agreement was the only option left.

Now the familiar, once soothing walls seemed to be closing in.

He sought the refuge of the open air; fleeing these confines, gaining the street, his gaze went skyward. Here stood a man whom, unbeknownst to his closest friends had been long the caretaker of a

132

hidden threat, a legacy, one now resurrected into poisonous life.

The promise he had made long ago threatened to overwhelm him – and reached out to claim one of his own.

Solvitur ambulando.

He set to pacing the street, eyes on anything, barely feeling the rough pavement under his boots.

His thoughts lingered on one thing alone now – Pen's words of scant hours prior – and the frightful sound in her voice.

He had come full circle, back into his house.

Frightful – for she's not afraid.

Chilling, for she envisions a cache of wisdom, of learning – a new world just waiting like the proverbial apple, for the right hand.

And she believes – she wants that hand to be hers.

Her words had come in a rush; how all the pieces had fit, how it was clear; all that was known about the author – his associations, his life and of those years of conjecture, how a man whose fame would move the literate world had seemingly vanished.

He could imagine her face, glowing, with excitement, with pride in accomplishment, as she relayed what she had found – and what she had deciphered.

All of which, silent and ardent in despair – her listener had already known.

"I know where it is, Percy, or I believe I do. There are few alternatives – for there the young Earl lived, there was the house whose foundations date from exactly the time when a book of this kind might well have found its way here, into the Abbey Library – from the East. From Persia has come so much of what we know now as ancient knowledge. Think of the legends, of stars, of spirits, of Djinns; all of it. The Wizard did not make this Book, of that I'm certain – and there may be more than one. But if it's still there, it is ready to come again into the light."

It was a desperate attempt that he made, to divert her, without revealing more.

"If it is what you say, Pen, I submit that *no one* can control this thing – *and no one should touch it*. Its power will not yield to anyone now living – *do not assume that it is neutral*. Such things will not be the servants of anyone."

"Nonsense; good is stronger than evil. I am good. I am strong. Good is *stronger* than evil."

Percy's eyes had gone again to his own walls; he referenced the need for the items displayed up there – and the spirit to use them, and more.

"No. *It isn't.*"

She had scoffed and demanded he ready himself – to go.

For go they must, she had said, and seeing now yet another threat, a new target for the forces moving amongst them – Percy Onslow had agreed.

That conversation was now past; unable to reach Monty or even Cass, he put his time to use.

Goaded by the certainty of battle and betrayal, the swordsman had assembled his gear. The warrior in him chose wisely; he was soon prepared. South they would go – south, and west, to the coast – where the caves hewed long ago by raging tides, that held this thing, most likely lay.

They would go; exactly as had the author of that quaint story long ago gone and seen unbelievable things – and imagined them into an Island, where sorcery and betrayal found their salvation in love.

They would find the place where good conquered evil.

Real life is not like that.

Good is not stronger than evil.

All was soon prepared; dawn's rosy fingers laced together across the skies – and Cass again came suddenly into his thoughts.

Percy went pale; his pack was lowered to the floor.

In sudden fear, he rushed back into the empty street, and there he stood, with a cold wind across his face and a chill in his heart.

The pale sky offered no respite to his dismay.

He was already running when, low and infinitely horrible, the blare of distant sirens broke the stillness of the fleeing night.

CHAPTER 15

THE WISE FOOL

Odd; odd and truly miraculous is my life – and the lives of many others, it would seem – right now.

Such were the thoughts of Montgomery Quist as he stood in the street before the Hythe residence for the second time that night.

As might have been that of the average lunatic, his gaze was upward, fixed on the setting moon. He was, however, far from average in any way; nevertheless, he was absorbed in the beauty of the waning satellite and plainly still overcome.

For by all right, I should not be alive right now.

The episode in the church several lifetimes ago had left a similar mark; the Cat had backed away from a man on his knees, ready if not willing to part with life. And once more had come intervention, supernatural if not divine.

Dear Heavens – and a lot more.

How are you still standing. And insanely – why are you still standing here?

Horrific, strident – the sound of the ambulance still rang in his ears. With only deep scratches on his face, and a great deal more bruises than he would admit, Quist stood watching those dreadful lights as they vanished into the dark.

It had been a very long night, indeed.

They had patched him up well. Yet, when his hand rose to his cheek, it came away with a gossamer smear of red.

Scars; I only hope Abigail's can outdo mine, and on both her feet.

She will do both, I know it; she will want the bragging rights.

He was unashamedly unsteady on his own limbs, but he turned finally and made his way back into the house. For, as the attendants had asked if he would come to the hospital, a voice had come, another fact made actual.

Here – you must remain here despite all – overcome, and remain.

He was still in the grip of horror, of fear for his friend – yet, in defiance of all reason, he had watched as the lady he knew and loved had been tended, and sent on her way, leaving a shocked and desperate academic to stand, torn in body and spirit – alone in the street.

Inside the house, he tossed back a double shot – and surveyed the wreckage.

His poor phone had had the virtue of life for just one call – that of securing aid. Then, it had literally come apart in his shaking hand.

Too much excitement, I'll wager, even for an Android.

138

Plus being flung ass over tea kettle across a very hard floor – and I can speak for the truth of that myself.

My landing square on top of it had had no effect, I'm certain.

The home lines were out as well; considering the degree of mayhem and the introduction of certain destabilising forces, this was also no surprise.

No; none at all. I'm somewhat surprised the house is still upright; that speaks for good bones, and sturdy ones at that.

He was already making light of a cataclysmic occurrence, the likes of which he sincerely hoped to never experience again.

He bent to pick up his battered cane – and it all came rushing back…

He clearly recalled saying it – 'what's that'.

It had been simple enough for, in the unnatural stillness of the room, a room where even the fire, in abject fear of the power of the dark – had shrunk down within the grate to leave the room darkened eerily beyond comprehension – there was still sound.

It came from the library doors, or rather from the gardens beyond, gardens just beyond the circle of light that the house had afforded.

Both of them had stared at the door – again had come sound and the door had indeed rocked in its jamb.

Then, many things happened and all at once.

Abigail Fitzalan had jumped up and leapt forward – the Orb rolled from her hand as Hell itself seemed to spring to life, tearing its animation from out of the very heart of blackness – and the Cat bounded into the library.

With a cry from the abyss, it slashed at Abby, sending her hurtling across the room.

Quist seized the fire iron and with a shout of terror and rage, the Professor struck as hard as he could at the demonic thing – then watched in horror as a flurry of sparks sprayed off the haunch of the creature as the iron savaged its fur.

The beast turned; with burning eyes, the Cat struck at him. Quist raised his arm in the nick of time – talons opened up his fine jacket sleeve, and caught him across the cheek.

He fell heavily; his phone bounced twice before hurtling across the room.

The stricken man looked up – bleeding, Abby had risen to her feet – now she took up her wand as the Cat charged her, seizing her shoulder in its massive jaws. The lady struck at the beast; still it dragged her toward the door – and the venerable scholar hauled himself up and yanked a still glowing brand from the fireplace.

He hurled the flaming log straight at the vicious killer.

With a howl and a savage shake, the Cat snarled and dropped its prey, and the stench of singed fur was rank in the room as Quist recovered his brand and struck again, and again. The Cat's swipe tumbled the man onto the floor – and its eyes blazed with blood lust.

Then it hissed – for Abby had reached the Orb – now she stood with the bright sphere and her wand in her hands.

The animal crouched; its maw was a mass of foam as Abby moved to place herself between the Hell Cat and the human— it readied to spring – to kill.

Abby's lips moved wordlessly – and from her wand's tip, a livid blue flame surged outward, to envelope both wand – and Cat.

The creature screamed.

It was the single most horrible sound that Quist could ever imagine as, with her legs giving way, with blood streaked across both face and arms and soaking her clothes, Abigail Fitzalan hurled the Orb at the beast.

It crashed onto the floor before the Cat, shattering into a fine powder.

Light erupted from the scattered grains; like a living wave it broke over the Cat – as the very fabric of what Monty would have formerly called the air *sheared* and ripped asunder.

Before his eyes, a *Gate* appeared.

141

From nowhere it grew and began to spiral – at its heart was nothingness – as dark and brilliant as the heart of a new made sun – what he saw was a whirlpool of blinding sapphire light, one that swirled madly, and the library became as cold as a crypt.

And the outline of the monster's form began to shiver and tear in Monty's sight – as the portal closed about the demonic thing.

With a sound like the voices of all the Furies combined, the creature roared – and its voice was swallowed up in the din of other voices, other howls – as the portal rippled – and began to close about the beast.

The hideous shape of the Cat was a maelstrom of shifting, writing darkness, one that was now growing smaller, and more dim – more distant, with each moment.

Spinning savagely, the Gate closed upon itself, vanishing into the air.

In a heartbeat, it was all over.

Gone was the Cat; warmth returned to the room.

Quist raised himself up long enough to see Abby slide to the floor.

She lay there, still as death.

Savaged and distraught, Monty's senses were reeling as he watched in frank terror – fascinated – as the scattered bits of shattered crystal began to *glow*. Then each *moved* as fragment after fragment sought its

142

fellow – sliding across the library floor – turning, joining, curling into new form, new life – and the Orb, solid and round, lay still before him.

Complete.

From the Orb came a brief but brilliant flash of pure light. Like a living star, fallen from the sky, the sphere blazed before the speechless man.

Then, the glow of the magical sphere lessened; the light dwindled to a soft luminescence – one of peace, of latent power – until there was just an Orb, clear and round and utterly motionless on the floor of the Hythe home.

All was as before.

And Montgomery Quist lowered his aching head, and knew no more.

He had roused to the uniquely dreadful sound of approaching sirens, to the ministrations of men and women who declared him bruised, a bit cut, but hale – and now, to the sight of a room sadly the worse for wear.

Along with her wand, the Orb he had secreted back to the desk. Aid had come and worked its own magic and left him, resolute and still wondering. He used his cane to steady himself as he stood over the desk where not one but two highly questionable objects waited, as proudly as prize heifers.

He waited as well.

And when the *voice* came from behind him, he turned not in surprise, but in satisfaction, for clearly this was why he was – as he had put it – insanely still here.

Then absolute shock took hold of him; he stood thunderstruck.

As if any shock could be greater than the events that had just transpired …

For here was One of whom he had heard much – One for whom all descriptions must pale beside the original standing calmly in the room with him.

"I know who you are," he said.

"Of course you do, and glad I am to see you on your feet," came the mild response. "Frankly I never thought she'd go after it."

Monty regarded the inexplicable One with yet unbridled wonder.

How long? How old?

And now – mortal? Or is He?

What reverence to I owe One who walked at the time of Christ?

Certainly respect, for Him and the Others, for we have the names – if not the faces – of thirteen, that all men called the Wise.

Those indeterminately coloured eyes regarded the academic, and Monty, who suddenly felt both infantile and twice his age, had the humility to blush.

"Sorry, old man – I mean, oh, dash it all! You see, I'm so used to studying the possible *existence* of the likes of You – or at least the tales, the legends. I have done so, calmly and objectively – and now that I see You in the *flesh* – it *is* flesh, I take it?"

The Master smiled as Monty forged forward.

"Well, You see, it's rather like popping over to the ATM and running into John the Baptist in the queue."

The Master now laughed; it was a warm, deeply human sound, and for an instant Quist forgot to be afraid.

The Master walked the room and stood before the mantel – there the smile of Iain Fitzalan shone from at least one of the images, whose frames had been lovingly worn by countless perusals.

"I quite understand; John was quite the fellow. I myself didn't have the privilege, but I know of One who did."

At the enormity of the implication, that of John being real, Quist's prodigious eyebrows furrowed.

"Ah. And is that One *still* …?

"Still alive?"

Silence held for a space.

"I'm not sure, if so – or not," the Master replied softly.

Monty pondered deeply; he had no more than a thousand or so questions, with the vast percentage right on the tip of his tongue.

But forbear, old fool.

By the grace of every divinity involved in this, there will be time – for lore, the like of which the world has never seen.

The Master's gaze was still on the portraits – one in particular – that of Iain, and Abby – and Randolph Hythe, and again, the scholar's imagination ran quite wild.

Dear Heavens, did Randolph know?

Had he always known – we know Iain went 'Below', he must have – did the Master and the man in the middle share a plan?

And what of Randolph Hythe?

The Master regarded the scholar; the scholar bore it as long as he could but those eyes, so bright, so piercing – in a moment, he lowered his own, wondering how, as he had obviously done so – the Sorcerer had borne such a gaze.

And he realised that the small talk was over.

"There's a great deal more to be done, isn't there?"

The Wise One nodded and His voice was soft.

"Do you want to *know* …?

Monty paled; it was the most normal, the most human of questions, as one started a journey that might prove …

"*No*," he replied staunchly – with a calm that surprised even himself.

"*Wise*. But remember *what you carry now* – home first."

"Yes, I will."

"Oh – and bring *that thing* that just came to mind."

Quist paled, then his cheeks went beet red.

Yet the great One smiled again.

"In addition to *the pipe*."

Monty held out his phone.

"Marvelous things; but don't worry – I'll take care of it."

The Professor stood flummoxed, much as had another man, a younger man for only a few moments, had stood, in anger, in defiance – in wonder.

"If You can do all this – why can't You fix all the rest of this Yourself?" he demanded.

"I never said I couldn't."

Monty felt a sudden inspiration.

"May I … go *with* You?" he ventured.

"No. It's too dangerous. I travel a different road – a faster one – *as I must*. I am sure you will forgive me."

One last try.

"Will I see You again?"

Now the One smiled broadly.

"You will ….*there*. And you will get there in time – *if you leave now*."

147

Monty gathered up his cane and his courage.

"Right. *There* – and we both know where that is – as will the others, I am sure."

There came a look of profound respect into the Master's eyes; then that gaze darkened, as seas do in the tight grip of storm – and Quist was reminded of another's eyes, eyes that flashed like these – steel dark, when moved by anger, despair …

Or passion – passionate courage, I would say.

The scholar looked long on the Master; that One did not hurry the man, nor did He speak.

And Quist took a deep breath; he studied that face for one more moment – then the man turned, collected his few things – looked all about the room one last time – and walked out the front door.

Stillness; the silence of a tenuous dawn, the precarious moment between *past* and that one next, *step* permeated the room.

Then the Master walked out the library doors – into the gardens, from where just hours ago, the Queen's servant and assassin had risen, with bloodlust in its heart.

The Master walked the space beyond; it was bordered by tall trees, and thickets of bay and sapling oaks, and the scent of thyme came up to His face as He trod the paths.

He halted – and took His wand from His jacket. The burled wood, tipped with ivory, set with silver shone, lay in His hand, polished and burnished to bright beauty.

And His words came low, resonant in the stillness that was now expectant – waiting – hearkening.

See air within the fire …Burn …

Last the Night.
Break the Day.
Wake the Sun, Wake the Moon.
All bindings through the Cosmos,
You are unto me!
A spirit of my own keeping,
As Master to Servant –
So it is – A Friend to a Friend!

The air moved – there came soft, barely discernible –a susurrance, as if the air itself were vibrating, and that rippling hush became a *tone* in the air.

And that tone was more *hiss than voice* …as the ground trembled.

The last of the cold moon looked down on the gardens, as wind forced the tops of the trees into shaking sway, shivering their tips, sending them into unholy dance.

Night birds, startled, rose calling into a sky still spattered with stars – cold was the air before the Mage who walked with the body of a man – as the world we do not see, the *hidden realm* wakened and rose from its dreadful slumber.

The Master stepped back.

Now He turned thrice in the garden – as thick darkness filled the space, as if all light – all life – were suddenly bound, extinguished, as if time itself hung silent and waiting.

For *something else* hung there – silent, black and waiting in the frigid space – hidden in a place *'between'*.

The Master's voice lowered, yet did it echo in the void that now reigned in the garden.

> *Smoke and fire – see Thy eyes.*
> *Brighter than a thousand skies,*
> *Of midnight black and moonlight bright.*
> *Hear My summons this dark night.*
> *As Thou didst fly and serve before,*
> *Come now at My Command – as yore.*
> *Do Thou this deed,*
> *And see it through …*
> *Thou hast Thy freedom – Life anew.*
> *Come … ARIEL ….*
> *Come … My Djinn.*

And a tremendous schism grew in the heart of the air before the Wizard.

There came a terrible *shear*, as light fell into darkness and into light again – as no colours and all whirled together in the tortured air – and the Sleeper,

150

the Hidden One, roused, and hungry – stepped through the rift, that space that drowses between life and death, dream and desire.

And the Djinn, the Lion of God – walked to stand before the Master.

About the Sprite, the air still burned in smokeless fire, and smoke curled and grew as the Being waited, with Its form changing from male to female to male, human to demon.

And the Eldest of those who had witnessed the Angels fight and fall, who had remained, thriving in the spaces between, that had stood at the command of men and gods, turned glowing eyes on the Wizard – and Ariel extended His hand.

The Master's fingers touched those of the Djinn and Ariel spoke.

"Thou hast no fear – like that Other One, so long ago."

"If My charms hold, Hidden One – My Ariel – as they have in the past," the Master replied.

"What is Thy bidding?'

"To follow Me – to reap the whirlwind, as before, to raise storm and sun, to cloak when darkness is needed, to keep those who must be kept – to do the deed at hand. Preserve the future, and gain Thy freedom."

The Djinn frowned; it was a ghastly look that passed across the features of ultimate beauty – ultimate good – and evil.

"That was promised before."

"This time it shall be given Thee."

The Djinn walked the space, as if Its limbs were unused to the dictates of this world. Then It turned, and looked to the house – and back to the Master.

"Someone comes, gentle Master."

The two returned to the library doors, they shut them against the day. Then thick darkness fell about Master and Djinn – and eclipsed and veiled, they watched.

For from the street, wending its way past the yellow tape, the scatter of coffee cups on the pristine Hythe lawns – a figure had just crossed to the front door.

The key in the bolt was unnecessary; the door opened – and with his pack in hand, Percy Onslow let the door close behind him and made his way to the scene of mayhem, of mystery and near murder.

The scent of singed flesh and fur came into his face. Onslow walked the floor and stopped over the spot where Abby had fought, and won a hellish battle.

A true warrior, he thought – and none but a few know even now the scope of her courage and strength. Be it so, that all shall learn soon – and not just at the end.

He picked up Quist's cap, left behind, forgotten in the wonder and awe of the last hour.

And hidden in darkness, a glow came to the Master's eyes, as He stood watching the swordsman – and Percy sensed that all was well, that the scholar was about and on his way somewhere – to where he would be needed.

Percy went round the room; he stopped over the desk, where a few items were lifted, and added to the pack he wore over his shoulder.

Then Onslow walked out the library doors, passing within a breath of the two who stood there, lost to sight – until he stood precisely where an unfathomable Being had stepped out from the living air.

In that freshness and lightness that precedes and follows close the dawn, the sword master took in the lingering scent of brimstone.

And he smiled again – and his thoughts were loud to those who watched, and the Master regarded the man with wonder.

Many have commanded Thee – those spirits that do run, those of the smokeless flame – those builders of temples, whose miracles – by the command of those who Serve *– serve all mankind. If that Spirit be true …*

The man pulled his jacket close against the autumn day; a flurry of leaves came across the walk, and scattered a light film of grey ash into the grasses, ash that was caught by the eager air, that turned sparkling, forming a cloud of many colours – and vanishing as if it had never been.

Percy stood for a moment – it was time for him to do the same.

He left the house.

And the cloak fell from the two in the garden.

The Djinn walked away from the house and turned to the Wizard – and extended Its arm.

"It is time," Ariel said.

And the Master joined the Djinn, and clasped Its hand – as smoke rose about the Sprite – the Fiend – the Friend – as smoke and fire engulfed the figures of both – grew blazing bright – and then vanished, taking the Master and the Servant with it.

CHAPTER 16

PASSAGE

Cold he was, chilled to the bone, as cold as the orts of earth lying there in the stone sarcophagus.

Caspian Hythe once again stood over the crypt where he had laid a lifeless body, of a young warrior, a young hero – and one so nearly in the direct line of Iain Fitzalan.

Here, with her blood-stained tunic, with her face white, and the life gone forever from those beautiful eyes – here she lay – with the Orb, the Eye of the First Gryphon in her cold fingers – as all our fates turned and the nightmare ended – and began again.

And here I stand once more – and my Knight stands beside me.

They had run; then sped from the Fitzalan house as though a demon might be hard upon them – with her red hair streaming behind, Ava Fitzalan led the way, followed by one who wished he had been wiser all along for so many months.

Wiser – and stronger – for my anger, my doubt has hobbled me.

And anger is the mind killer; since that day at the Castle ruins, where I failed – for too long I have been that angry man.

Stronger I needed to be – not more powerful, which is not the same thing, not the same at all.

The young woman had led, steadfastly refusing all his enquiries. He, with a full heart and a burning need to know followed Ava, and her nearness fascinated him as never before.

Since that night in the cemetery, at the side of a cold, white crypt, at the grave of a man whose tales had somehow roused and fed a great Evil.

There in the nave of the ruined church, moonlight passed through a shred of the still steadfast glass of another age – and the light split, shining in the crypt – riven into many colours.

And words came to him; Abby's words came back.

A cloak.

Just hours ago, in secret, this night – and it had been ages, truly, since that other night when the Undine, with fire in Her eyes – had spoken to him, back in the distant past.

Then as now, there had been moonlight; it had flooded across the Silent Pool as the Elemental, *unbound*, had revealed Her soul laid bare, the scope of Her enchantment, its savagery – intoxicating and seductive.

'Lest Brother mar what Brother hold … a Prince shall rise, where none has been.'

And did She not warn of a Book … and a Cloak of many colours?'

Has this same thread, woven long ago, come now, before Carroll ever lived, did it travel from the past, to the land 'Below', for not one but two life lines – to bring us again to the brink?

Was it Carroll's mythos alone – I think not – and now I ask why I am only seeing now that possibility of events.

He envisioned a legacy of Power starting from the past, in defiance of a *chain* forged by a dark Power, then and now – waiting and eager.

To 'now' – where I lay hands on the next link in that long chain.

And Ava knows, I see that she has always known – as we stand together in this place of unholy rest, of death – and of rebirth…

They had left the car and without hesitation, the Knight had led the way into the ruined church.

And Cass followed, spellbound by her, as he had been from the beginning – for the one who led was different somehow – more enigmatic, more compelling than ever before.

New- found power – when I look into her eyes, the sense of hidden, nascent power is overwhelming.

Inside, all was still, and at the altar stone – still a Gate, still sleeping, now the Sorcerer looked down, not on vacant ancient soil but on the affirmation of a brutal past.

He regarded the Knight; she had led him here as surely as …

157

Now he stared at her.

"How do you know about this place."

She turned to face him, there in the near dark.

"Why here, Ava? How *exactly* did you get back here – from *'Below'*? I couldn't do it; how did you? Did you use this portal?"

She took a step toward him – he stepped back, away from her.

"No."

"It's been months for me, Ava. I lost my future, everything I had here, and found it again in the past – with your father."

She took a deep breath.

"For me – it was an *eternity 'Below'*– and I *know what you did, what you accomplished.*"

"*How?* How could you possibly know – was it Abby – you didn't come to find me …"

The Knight's voice was harsh, terrible, and she stalked away from him.

"Cass – *please.*"

In a fury, he went after her.

"Tell me the *truth*, damn it! Can't you just tell me – or won't you! Tell me the truth!"

Now she whirled about, livid with anger – and something more – for the dim light in the church *changed* somehow.

"*I swear* – on *her* life – and *mine* – what I did, *what I do now* – may save us all, without shame or stain, either of crime or dishonour! *That's the only truth I can give you!"*

"That's not enough!" he snarled and he ran to her and seized her by her shoulders.

"Get off me!"

"I won't! Don't you see – I died that day, and every day since – and *this* is all you have to say?"

With all her strength, Ava Fitzalan struck the Sorcerer full in the face.

Thunderstruck – at the brutality – the force of the strike – he fell backward onto the hard stones of the floor – and the Knight stood over him, with literal fire in her eyes – and both fists clenched.

He glared up at her – his fingers went to his lip and came away wet with blood.

"Don't try that again."

"I will if I must."

He started to rise …

"Stay down!" she commanded.

"Make me."

The Knight's eyes glittered hard – deep within them stood sharp appraisal – coupled with a strange, dark humour – and pride – and it came to him in a flash.

She's testing me.

This is all a test; I am being judged by what I do now.

The Knight watched the Sorcerer. The Sorcerer rubbed his chin – then slowly rose to his feet.

Ava stood firm; only when Cass' breath came under his control did she speak.

"I didn't come to you because I couldn't. I can give no answers to you right now – because I can't."

Her voice changed; at the desperate plea he heard now, his guard dropped.

"Hear me, Mage – hear – *and see*. What I do now – I do without choice. Like a crossbow shot – so do all our lives depend on speed – and accuracy. If you cannot be with me – you must step aside – *or I must make you.*"

Moments sped while the two regarded one another, until he asked.

"What must I do."

For a second he thought she would touch him, but she stepped back – and the stone floor moved beneath them.

The entire ancient edifice shuddered.

Bits of the still remaining roof clattered down as the floor trembled again, and against a sky torn between night and dawn – lightning flashed in majestic brilliance in the sky.

And the Knight's words came low and portentous.

"The earth cries out – in woe. You and I – and others perhaps must travel with all speed. And the earth itself must help us now … my Sorcerer."

It had been long since he had worked what little magic he remembered.

How is it that I know – that she herself can do this thing – yet I must?

He walked past her, out of the church, to a spot where his steps seemed to catch and hold in the turf.

She followed then let him stand alone.

Alone – beside the edifice, pale light etched the skies. Night still held beneath the boughs of the high trees that ringed this place – and Caspian Hythe fought the memory of another time, when he stood here clutching the one dear to the Fitzalan line.

And to me as well – for with the death of the sword master Alesia – the path of my own future and the return of the Knight was assured.

Song came from the forest; the woodlands were awakening, and the sharp muted calls of the owls slashed through the damp air.

The Sorcerer took out his wand.

He studied it, the fine wood, the workings, the designs in glowing metal across its surface.

Then he knelt and laid the beautiful thing on the wet turf.

A sudden calm fell upon the space – the attending dawn halted, arrested in her path, her colours vivid but static in the queerly darkening heavens.

All was still beside the ruined church – and the spirit of Caspian Hythe stood waiting – as the world around him came to a standstill – and the storm left his soul – replaced by a Song.

It rose from the earth beneath his boots, and the Mage hearkened to the murmur of water, delving deep and traversing the lands below, to the rhythm and restless burgeoning of the grass, to the muted chorus of root and trunk, the coaxing calls of leaf to green leaf.

He heard the sigh of stones yet unmade merge with the shrill lament of those dissolving, as they joined the eternal river that was the undying Song of the living earth.

And he stood transfixed, spellbound, until there was no longer a man standing on the darkling vale – but one who, in strength and power – had given himself again – and was One with the Song.

From the earth itself, from deep within the Sorcerer, the Word came to him – dulcet, enthralling, and imperative.

> *You slumber not; You slumber deep.*
> *The wealth of earth is Thine to keep.*
> *Come now – Oh, GNOME,*
> *Heed Thou my prayer,*
> *Rise up, return – to Sun and Air,*
> *Where I stand now, let Spirit live;*
> *With Power and Might –*

Thy Presence give.
Oh, hear me Master – grant this plea.
Quit Thou Thy realm – and Come to me.

What began as a low rumble became a deafening tumult, a roar of all the senses.

The earth rocked, as across a sky hung between the twin poles of night and day – lightning flashed again in violent *accord*.

The earth split beside the Mage; a chasm of light, diamond bright, of darkness blacker than iron gaped, opened at his very feet.

And the Sorcerer – one with the spirit of the Elemental that ruled all domains below, under whose might the oceans answered, rushing in to fill the chasms He created – slid to his knees before the One rising up.

Brighter than star light were the stones encrusting the Gnome's hair, as brown as new turned earth.

Wide were His shoulders, powerful the arms that commanded the earthquake, by whose hands the highest mountains rose, shaking off the poor weak clutch of sleeping stone.

With his hair matted with sweat, his face pale and every limb trembling, Cass knelt – before the Master of gem and ore – the One by whose leave all life may continue, under whose cherished care – all

163

green things slept, and dreamt, and healed to rise into life.

The air was perfumed, filled by the incense of the ages, of spices gathered, of the heavy rich sweetness of living forest, of towering pine and hoary oak.

An emerald green billow laid about His massive shoulders as, with a sound louder than that of the avalanche – the Gnome set His sturdy foot upon the splintered earth.

Ava Fitzalan came forward; for the space of many moments, the Elemental regarded the Knight – and her eyes did not lower beneath that steely gaze.

And then the Knight knelt beside the Mage.

Yet a look of recognition flashed across the robust features of the Gnome – then His bright regard fixed itself upon the Sorcerer – and that regard was stern.

"Thou hast come at last, Mage – to seek passage – and for now, passage is denied."

Aghast, the Sorcerer gazed up at the towering entity – for if they could not secure the Gnome's help, his heart told him they would be lost.

"Nay – not lost – but hear – and see."

An ancient Place – and close beside,
A grotto – Dost Thy doom abide?
The earth itself cries out in woe,
Into my Realm, so deep below,

164

That moon and tide so grey and frore,
Embattled rest, reft of their Power.
The sea descends – the Book revealed,
Thy fates – and His – and All, are sealed.

I fear thee, Mage, for Thou art weak,
Hast Thou the strength to havoc wreak?
If charms and riddles rest obscure,
Upon Thine own reaps vengeance sure.
A test of Three – all fortunes fade,
Find Thou – within, Thy courage made.
Return – It waits on unknown sands,
Then passage take – from Mine own hands.

The Sorcerer rose to his feet; Ava followed as he backed away from the Elemental – and that One's glowing eyes followed him, measuring, appraising – judging.

A sudden sense of alarm filled the Mage – he stood stock still beside the Knight, and her look was, like his, one of alarm.

In the next moment it came.

Hard upon the silence, rousing the sounds and voices of forest and meadow into terrified life – loud, in direst warning – echoed the shrill harsh tones from Cass' phone.

CHAPTER 17

IN HOSPITOR

Never play the instrument – always play the song.

So much, so fast, I'm beyond the capacity for the next curve ball.

Or am I.

Low, soothing; as all hospital lighting should be – in soft light, Percy Onslow turned away, and Cass sensed it was due to much more than the sight of his friend in the bed.

Much more than the bombshell of knowing, of finally telling so much more than I had even an inkling of.

Much more than even having to call me, of not being able to reach Quist, to even satisfy himself that the old man was still alive.

Yet he is; somehow, I can feel that – and I'm certain Ava can too.

The Mage regarded the Knight.

Her hand had gone to Percy's shoulder — the swordsman was still distraught, his mind clearly absorbed in matters yet undisclosed.

What he knows – has known and done – it has weighed heavily on him – and there is more.

He is afraid now, deeply – about what comes, what has just happened.

Onslow's grip on his calm, ever- present and always so reliable was grievously fragile; Cass' heart went out to him. Ava turned back to the Mage, meeting his regard with apology in her eyes and that still intoxicating dry humour on her lips.

The Sorcerer's eyes went from one to the other; then he shook his head. Flummoxed, angry; but that anger was fast fading away.

There was no longer any time for accusation; all that mattered were the next steps.

"If I did not love the two of you as much as I do – I'd bloody well bash both your heads together."

Percy smiled grimly.

"Well deserved. I must say, the task of 'training' the likes of you, and yet keeping silence – have been the hardest things I've ever put my hands to. Forget the swords; this may very well be my masterpiece."

He didn't need to add 'his final one'; all days were numbered now, all lives and fates poised on the edge of one of those famed blades...

On the heels of Percy's frantic call, the Knight and the Mage had sped away from the church grounds.

They had not waited to watch as that Elemental there had begun to fade from sight.

Slowly, then with greater and greater speed, the Gnome's form became indistinct, as the outlines

168

of His powerful limbs began to merge with the growing light of dawn.

The diamonds scattered throughout His flowing hair kept their brilliance to the last, and to the last, even as Cass and Ava raced away – the Elemental's eyes glowed with emerald and gold; earthy and penetrating was the gaze that fixed and stayed on the humans, until they were lost to mortal sight.

But not to His.

For as all his kin, He shared the Vision of All – of all the earth, all its denizens. His sight encompassed all their doings, and their transits fell, in part, under His demesne.

His powers over the earth were unimaginable, and over its fundamentals and legacy – incomprehensible. All these were part and parcel of His realm, and were charged to Him.

But not to Him alone.

For at its borders, those strange, ephemeral, ill-defined boundaries where earth and water and sky shared dominion—His Voice was *heard* – and His authority joined with Those who governed each direction, each dimension. His Voice was great; His reach monumental – and inescapable.

Wary, aloof and incalculable, only the Being who ruled fire – He alone remained distinct – Salamander, the One of Fire.

Yet His faculties reached furthest, into the souls of stars and of men.

For the spark of life finds its source in elemental fire. In fire are the stars born, with fire does the lightning draw its bolt across the heavens.

And at the very heart of Spirit – there, too is the spark – of life, of enlightenment – of courage in the face of impossible odds.

None of this touched those at the bedside.

Cass now looked down on the lady in the bed.

Her wounds had been dressed. Despite the assurances of the staff, despite his sensations of the small but desperately needed signs of her continued progress – he saw only one thing.

Aunt and mother in turn; yet neither.

Abby – in danger, for she is.

Still threatened, for the enemy is still about.

Dearest – one I can't bear to lose.

Unassisted, her breathing was shallow but strong. She had awakened long enough to see and smile weakly at Cass – that smile had gone straight to her eyes as she had caught sight of Percy – and then of Ava Fitzalan close beside him.

Abby's lips had mouthed the Knight's name. Then suddenly Abby's hand had reached for the daughter of Iain Fitzalan – and the Knight had come close, crouching by the bed to take Abby's hand – and bring it to her lips.

Whatever she had known or not known of that lady, the young woman had kissed her on the forehead. Then Abby closed her eyes, slipping away into a sleep so deep it was like that last one, one that they all had feared.

The three had left her then, taking their way through the halls, where others lay in rooms, never imagining the wounds, the battle – that this one warrior had endured, survived – and won.

The wanderers found refuge in an alcove, private and still, one with windows opening out onto the green of a courtyard. The three stood together – and full day began to break.

Cass was still wordless; the discovery that the Master was now in his world was staggering to him.

For Ava had not been the only one who had surmounted the terrible cataclysm trapping her *'Below'*.

Or 'Between' – for he knew now that the Master had come into the 'now'.

Into a life like my own; and only now do my doubts ease, my doubts of myself – my integrity, my virtue – those doubts are now fading.

I will see – where the real danger lies, and has lain.

The Master – above. Suspected – I should have guessed – for I felt it. New power – did He bring her across with Him – when I couldn't?

And why?

Who – or what – did I raise?

It was a new day, and Percy Onslow began to speak urgently, answering the questions not yet asked – for time was only one enemy and sight and speed were imperative. He spoke of things beyond what had transpired in the distant past, beyond the conspiracy – to the 'now', where the danger had always lain, sleeping – ready to awaken into new and terrible life.

As the new day dawned, he spoke – of the Abbey – of the Library – of the rise and evolution of the Place House.

How against all odds a Star Taker, a very special and unusual one, had found its way West – to be broken into pieces so that a terrible Thing – one that had every appearance of a Book – might more easily remain hidden – and helpless.

How the Taker did not only direct the way; how Fitzalan himself, that great scholar, that historian and linguist, fearing the worst, had left clues that might be discovered – to take the path back – in place and time – to the Gateway, to the clues to where the portal had been sequestered.

"It was a place far from the greed, and the arrogance of men, far from their foolishness – in wishing, in believing that any one person could control the Thing. For Caspian – you must believe me – no one can."

Percy paced the alcove, then he turned and his face was terrible.

172

"And now comes Tam – a prince – or a Demon – I don't dare guess which."

At those words – prince or demon – Cass scowled, for he had heard that referenced before by the side of a mere when rose the guardian, sovereign and servant of all flowing waters – and She had warned him.

'Lest Brother mar what Brother hold …A Prince shall rise …'

The Mage's gaze grew flint bright, his eyes stormy and dark.

"How do *you* fit here – in all of this."

The swordsman looked away; then he turned and walked to the windows.

Outside, birds made their morning song among the green leaves – leaves that would soon turn – and begin to fall.

Already the light of the year had begun to change. Softened, more golden, it streamed with a gentler, more pensive intensity, with less purpose.

"So all light might fail in the end," he murmured. "If purpose fails …"

He had spoken very softly, but his words stayed long with the Mage and the Knight.

"It was long ago. The Taker – and perhaps the Book itself, bound and locked – came from the East. The Lion Heart brought many trophies from those lands, lands which were strange and distant in everything except the then greatness of their ideas, of

173

their ideals, of philosophy, science – and knowledge. My own ancestor buried one piece of the Taker in the Pool. Another lies waiting – at the ruins of the Abbey itself. And the third – I fear – is now in the hands of the enemy."

Now the Sorcerer paced in alarm as Percy spoke.

"Bound in gold, chained by spells of power, the Book was separated from the Taker – sent to the Abbots at Place House, near to the sea. There it would be hidden – hardly noticed – kept safe – apart."

Percy Onslow turned back to the two silent with horror.

"But there is no safety in ignorance. The Book, still bound, was taken – drowned, even as the playwright contrived in his tale – and there it waits."

"Percy – if all the pieces were united, put together …"

"The Taker points the way – the way to the Book, and to open it. It also completes the path – for the Book to rise – and open."

Now Ava stepped forward.

"Then it is a real Book?"

"As real as the apple was in that Garden long ago. It lies ready for the first hand – the pages are doors, hungry to open into new life. And not all those doors are to buried treasure."

The Knight burst out.

"*Tam has a piece*. Any friend of the Cat has power – he will try to use it."

"Tam is *insane*," Percy said.

"God help us – *he isn't*," she replied.

Cass went to the man who had trained him, had guided, and advised him, a man of fidelity, of constancy – of courage coupled with a mighty will.

"Onslow, look at me. This Book – is it the only one?"

And the sword master's eyes locked with those of his student.

CHAPTER 18

GRYPHON

The sky above suddenly darkened.

The wind was rising suddenly, sending a billow of leaves, both dry and lifeless, and green and hale, across the panes – and a rain of hail slammed hard against the window where the three stood.

The birds in the courtyard grew silent; the swordsman looked long on Cass – and Ava, to whom he handed a small leather bag.

And the Mage wondered.

Was this the last time?

Percy came to stand close to his student, his teacher – his friend.

"Cass, I've seen a good deal since the day Fitzalan graced me with his wisdom. It comes to me now that the symbols we have, that we hold dear – these may be *hidden* sometimes. *But they are there* – and they are there to save us. Look for me – at the end."

The sword master picked up his small pack.

"Percy, wait."

But the sword master turned on his heel and quickly walked away.

177

There was no time to follow; loud and startling, a low clap of thunder resounded in the alcove. Clouds scudded again over the building, chased by the sun – and by something massive, something in swift flight – and an eerie shadow sped across the grounds of the courtyard.

Storm clouds surged high above them—and then there came the *sound*.

The two remaining in the alcove looked up – to the ceiling above and wonder was on their faces.

For what they both clearly heard was the sound of some heavy thing scrambling across the roof.

"That roof is two stories above us," muttered Cass. "How can we possibly hear that?"

Furtive, wary but insistent, the sound came again.

"Expect the unexpected," advised the Knight. "Let's go."

They left the room; there was no sight of the swordsman in the hall.

No sign of anyone – and at the closest door that might have given access above – they halted.

"It's open."

"Of course it is."

Cass looked in – and up the stairs. Again; a deserted hall – and an open door.

"I still wonder how it is that we're able to do this, to get up here?"

She laughed.

"You can't seriously be asking that."

That ready door shut behind them with a solid snap – forward they must go.

And upward, to the roof, where the two passed cautiously through yet another open door – and stepped out onto gravel, wet and cold with hail.

He saw that Ava wore a dagger – and he was, as ever, always armed. Yet neither drew, as they stood there.

Waiting.

Gone was the night.

The wind was seriously cold in their faces, bracing with the first touch of winter, and at its back, Cass tasted the salt tang of the sea.

Suddenly that wind rose again, then just as abruptly died, and a ray of purest light, of warm sunlight pierced the clouds and beamed down upon the two – and the One that now strode regally into view.

The Knight stepped forward, and immediately dropped onto one knee – before the creature that did not exist – and her father would have been proud to see the light that came from Gryphon's eyes as it regarded the young woman.

"My Lord, we come as bidden, in deepest respect – and need."

It had been a long time since Caspian Hythe had seen this creature, in his own past, in the greater past of others – and once again he was speechless.

In need, and desperate, for here again is Gryphon, Guide and Guardian of Fates – and futures.

Like leaves of beaten copper, the feathers on the great head lifted in the wind and the beast turned from the one kneeling – to the Sorcerer.

It padded forward, its withers nearly hip high. The heavy talons caught and raked on the gravel as it strode to meet the man – and Cass knelt before the messenger, even as he had in vision, before his journeys *'Below'*.

Imponderable, the enormous eyes of green, and russet and gold were a marvel – like to those of bird and cat combined – and those saucer like orbs fixed on the Mage.

And this time, that man met the creature's searching gaze, and, as it had before – much of the world around Cass grew dim as the Gryphon's words, its very thoughts came to him.

I see into thy heart, Mage; thy need, thy fear – indeed it is not finished.

For what began before thy birth, from the rash creation to the passage of the Book of Wonders – that menace prevails, and will touch us all.

For the Wise are such in many things, except in Their own frailty, as men, as brothers.

And the Wise are first and foremost the children of men, even as art thou and thy Knight.

So it was that a great sorcery begat a greater peril – and greed, rivalry and death followed this Thing. Know now that it was Brother against Brother, as the Wise contrived and schemed and dissembled –and Two were bound in wroth.

But ever hungry, ever seeking and following the lure of Power, That which was awakened 'Below' – in thy time – found Its way into the carnage, abetted it, and grew strong – in treachery, in lies – in false promises.

Cass froze.

The Queen – the Queen.

And Cass looked into the eyes of that mysterious hybrid and looked deeply, as a single word came into his mind.

Onslow.

The Gryphon's eyes glowed.

Aye; a master swordsman, that and more, Mage. Boldly did he venture where more than one had already come – 'Below'.

Boldly did he seek me out, and he beheld the sword, that blade which still speaks to both past and future – the Blade that Binds.

Girdled with the runes of power, he saw – even as did thy Knight's sire – the crux deep within the blade, that which has faded yet awaits the time of its arrival.

Thus may the darkest of forces move those of light – for absolute Being is the sum of the two.

181

And he took up the blade, and balanced it in his bare hands – and Fate turned on its coin – and moved forward. For far too great a battle loomed, for the way to be held by just one.

And the Sorcerer's mind flew.

It had been Abby who had sent him to Percy, to choose and recover that sword, to learn its ways, to take it to face the trial in the past – to return again.

Yes, Mage – to return to thee.

That sword revealed a riddle, a message, with words it did exclaim – that which will serve thee now.

The Mage pondered; for he bore no sword now, and the beast's eyes glittered on the dagger he wore.

The very earth cries out in woe – for thee.

Ready thyself – return to Him, who is the Master of the Earth – for what is to come. Three are tested – three shall fall …

> *Three are tested; three shall fall,*
> *Below the waves, in chasms deep,*
> *Find there the well where portals sleep.*
> *A brother's blood, a final key –*
> *With just the Third – 'twill Open be.*
> *In pain – in loss, thy choice is all,*
> *For three are tested – three shall fall.*

The creature's voice fell to a whisper; Cass roused as Ava came beside him – and Gryphon's final warning rang in his mind.

Return, Mage.

Thy passage awaits – to lose all is to gain all – if all is given.

The creature turned away; in dismay, the Sorcerer gained his feet, and the Gryphon flicked its massive wings once, looking back at the two on the roof, with their hearts as cold as their hands.

Once more, the enormous liquid gaze passed over them both.

Then, the fabulous creature began to run, nearly invisible in its speed – it raced across the roof and the giant wings spread wide as it took to the air.

It needed but three heartbeats; the Gryphon was lost to view – and a savage gust rose, sending small dry leaves billowing in gloomy flight across the gravel.

As if seeking the answer to one last question, Cass and Ava stood silent for many moments.

The Knight stared at the point in the sky where the remarkable One had vanished into the clouds.

"Is He ever wrong?" asked the Sorcerer.

"No. But His words – and their true meaning – are always subject to interpretation."

And Ava Fitzalan turned and stood before him, and that cold, uncertain wind lifted her hair, sending it into a halo of flame as the sun breached its prison and streamed down again.

183

"Will that be enough for you?" she murmured.

He looked long on her.

"It will have to do. Come on."

They gained the street, and then the way back.

It took less time than one could imagine, to return to the ruined church.

The earth bore little sign of the Gnome's rising; Cass made his way to stand finally at the spot where the Elemental had trod upon these upper lands.

Wind whispered about the place; lonely and poignant was this setting to the Mage. Ancient and vaguely horrible it still seemed from the time before, to this time, the one of return.

Yet if I cannot outpace the horror – I cannot serve.

The clouds lowered; thunder made welcoming chorus in the distance.

Both the Sorcerer and the Knight stood rooted in their place – as the branches of the trees about the devastated church moved – against the wind.

Creaking and groaning, their boughs lowered and rose, in obeisance to the One who ruled their roots and crowns. Here came the One whose Song ran in their twigs and sap, who set the sweet melody of water and air, to meet and join – bringing green life to the woods and the world – and the Gnome took

184

form from the leaves and shadows of the trees – and strode toward them.

And the Gnome's rich voice, like that of rustling leaves and gently sliding stones, rang out in the space before the trees.

> *Seek Thou …A Place,*
> *Where brush and bracken turn,*
> *With knots about the battered Urn.*
> *A portal waits, now that Thy*
> *State avows Thy passage – Seize*
> *Thy fate!*
> *Thy passage take from Mine own hands,*
> *Seek Thou the Thing in drownéd lands.*

And the Elemental held out His hands to them.

Gnarled they were – as the roots that bend their way down, deep into His realm. Young and hale they were, as bright as new growth, tender and crisp that opens in blind hope, to stand fast against the final snows and ice of spring.

And the Sorcerer gazed at Him.

"Master – *I come to serve.* In Thy name – and in the name of all Thou hast wrought – of all that falls to Thy protection – guide me – guide us now."

On his hand, the Mage's ring glowed, as he reached out to take hold of the Gnome's hand – as did the Knight.

There came a shock that drove the breath from Cass' chest – to Cass it felt as if a landslide had come alive, to bury, crush and claim him.

He heard the Knight cry out – and in the Mage's mind came glacial ice and the searing heat of molten lava, all at once. He heard the roar of living trees and leaves, the groan of rock and ore as they burgeoned into life – the life of the Living Earth.

Icy cold, a cold too harsh to breathe – as the Gate opened under the spell of the Elemental; and the ground opened under their very feet.

Through endless caverns moist with moss and leaves, the pure cleansing scent of churning life engulfed them. They fell through space, through the very heart of the earth itself as the Gnome *asked* – and made free the Passage.

Searing cold at his heart, within his bones – then came the shearing snap as they passed through earth and void – and Caspian Hythe knew no more.

CHAPTER 19

SEEDS

"You're late."

The face across from him was still evanescent, like a stream of champagne bubbles caught and swirling in a glass. The eyes in that face blazed brighter for a second; Tam had never been able to determine their colour – not since the beginning.

That beginning had been a long time ago. Albeit dimly, he still remembered the day when he had first heard that Voice – calling him from the house.

I couldn't have been more than five. Yet, there it was, sonorous, resonant, a whisper as soft as a murmur on the wind.

But clear.

What he had heard, in body and mind had been the simplest of summons – his own name.

But the command had been clear.

Unable to ignore it, to resist – he had pulled himself up from the fine oak floor. His game had been forgotten; the colourful little ball was left behind in the house – it was just a house, for at no time, nor in any place he had been – had he ever felt at home.

And he had been in many places.

187

That day, out he had gone, making a child's hesitant way through the door left ajar, stumbling a bit down the brick stairs – into a summer garden with the scent of new flowers and the hum of bees all round him.

So had another Garden once seemed, when mankind was young and innocent. But there – as well as here, the minds and hearts of the innocent might be swayed – cajoled by darker, more insidious forces.

For the price of innocence is ultimately temptation; the pitfall of innocence is its ultimate lack of preparation – against persuasion, against seduction, against evil.

And there was no one to protect him, no one to fling up a barrier on this very sunny day – against the dark.

Whatever else they had done or not done, those whom at first he had called father and mother – and later uncle and aunt – they had kept him well. Bright, inquisitive, with a curiously purposeful look in his eyes, he had thrived. Years would pass before he would first suspect, and then learn he was not of this family – not directly at least – before he would hear the truth.

That truth would come from an unlikely source, and late – but he would suspect it far before.

Clear to me, clear to all who knew me – my differences were always too great.

Their world – that superficial, flat and simple one I shared with those around me – it was always so small – too small.

My true legacy was greater, more especial, and I would quickly aspire to a far greater one.

For then, as in years before – there had always been the Voice.

Rich in tone, soft in execution; that day it had been a bare whisper that had somehow reached him in the house – one that grew more potent, yet not louder as he had left the garden path and pushed his way into a thicket.

Here, and beyond – the gardeners had lessened their efforts to curb the natural wildness of mature trees and dense shrubs. It was a riot of green around him, far from the reach of untangled civilisation back at the house.

Had this been any other boy, it would have been incredibly dangerous. As it was, he was young, no one had seen him leave – he was small.

To all appearances, he was alone.

Unfortunately, had he been *truly* alone, the danger would have been far less.

The thicket gave way to an open space ringed with tall hedges and even taller trees. Like giants they seemed to the little boy as he stood, surrounded by them – and there he had waited.

I'm glad you've come.

Male and female, both and neither – it was a Voice pleasant to hear.

Startled, the waif had turned about. There was thick shade under the boughs of the giant trees about the space, and from deep within that shade – eyes now looked out, regarding him gently.

His nanny had just been reading to him, spinning a tale from her own past, all about the ancient spirits of the trees, of the oaks and elms whose lives and spirits might intersect with others.

So had he, in all innocence, assumed that here in the glade, a tree spirit had elected to communicate with him.

Lucky lad.

Upon being bidden, Tam had sat himself down upon a atone. There, for more than an hour, he had chatted with the one hidden in the grove, chatted most pleasantly.

When the boy had asked when the spirit might come out – to play – the Voice had hesitated, then replied very softly.

It is not yet time; I am still bound – but soon—I may be stronger, strong enough to be with thee.

Then thou shalt see Me clearly – as I see thee.

Tam had been well pleased.

Making his way back to the house, he was enthralled – he had found a companion, very wise, very gentle and one who had promised great things.

In the months that followed, the little one grew more pensive, more polite – more distant. For he had promised to return to the glade, and he had kept that promise. His human family could only remark upon it, how one day the captious, stubborn little boy had been absent for an hour and had returned much changed.

A fair amount of time had passed since then. Years swept by; the Voice had never left, never ceased its gentle advice – its less gentle demands.

And he had been guided and most importantly seconded by a scarcely seen presence from first a grove of trees, then elsewhere. The young man that was had long ceased to question the impressions shared so willingly with him.

Hungry for knowledge – for power – for significance – he had learned to do well what came so naturally to him. He had used that time well, those years well, elaborating on the ideas, the concepts – the arts – of the One in the grove.

The Art; in essentials… and so much more.

And no longer merely different, he had become divergent.

The Voice had never commanded malevolence; it had urged voracity – for power, for dominion. It had never exhorted cunning – it had never cultivated disdain for the lives, the very existence of others.

Those endowments Tam had discovered and nourished himself, until the promises rendered to him at birth, had flourished into potency.

He had come far; in feeling, in desire, in power and in distance from that sunny glade on that golden afternoon.

From where he stood now, in half-lit silhouette, Tam looked up.

Arching high above his head, the sweeping stone ceiling of the wide vault curved effortlessly.

Near collapse threatened the edifice above. Yet here, in the vaults, sturdier stone had endured, unfazed by the wrath of time, virtually untouched by the discord and strife of many centuries.

Old churches, especially very old ones, were often famed not just for their outer glories of carved stone and marvelous glass.

Far below, their catacombs were often as resplendent – holy or otherwise – as those towering walls that soared above, that lifted the fingers and hearts of man closer to divine mercy.

But mercy is an unpredictable thing; it can be found in odd, utterly unforeseen places and events.

Walls could fall, and did. Roofs were sundered by storm, split by the works of man, or lightning – or by forces more sinister, less explicable.

Not so easily, the vaults.

Not so these vaults.

So it was that this young man stood now, as he had countless times before, in the spaces that still spread, inviolate and unplumbed.

He stood so directly below the floor where sat a stone altar in a ruined church, where a desperate old man had found a ring – one that would turn the tides of fate. Where that old man had faced down a demonic threat.

Time had been short, as had been the recompense in the project. Those who had excavated the ravaged church had limited their delving to the grounds about the place and the nave – where Caspian Hythe, in another time, had laid a still warm body in a cold sepulcher.

They had done better to have searched the structure itself … *'Below'*.

For Tam stood on unhallowed earth.

Silent and sleeping, a Gate lay here – he could feel it. He had seen it open – as the Cat had ventured up to join him – and the curious footprints in the dust attested to the access of monstrosities of other kinds.

For now, a pair of indeterminately coloured eyes narrowed in the gloom – fixed once more on Tam, the apprentice – even as had been Caspian Hythe. There was grim humour edged with taunt in that Voice echoing in the space lit by torch, electric and other wise.

I am never late.

And conversation had followed, intricate and long, until Tam was ready.

He turned away from that swirling glow that circled in the dark just beyond the light of the candles he now refreshed. The eyes followed the young Wizard, carefully, benevolently – hungrily – until Tam turned back to their regard; for the long conversation was nearly over.

"I miss the Cat."

Of course you do. He will rise again – when the thing is recovered – when the deed is done.

"I know; a brother's bond …"

Both thine and Mine.

"Shall I pass through?"

No; there is work for thee on the road.

And now a new ally stands ready to thy hand.

"And to Thine?"

Always. For they are weak – and we are strong.

And very soon – we shall both be stronger still.

CHAPTER 20

FULL OF NOISES

Well, if this isn't just another little bit of attic space 'Below' – I don't know what in Hell is.

Dark were the thoughts of the scholar as he stood at the interface of his world, and one that promised to be infinitely more monstrous.

I am much too old to be doing this. Any of this.

No, I really mean it this time.

I've said it too many times in the last few months – why am I cursed with repeating myself.

The answer was obvious.

Because you are still an old fool – and still here.

It had taken him a disturbingly short time to reach the coast – to get as close as he could to where he intended.

Where I intend to disappear …

He had actually seen it in passing – the Tychfield Abbey, now Tichfield Abbey, or rather what remained. It was of course no longer an Abbey, not for centuries. The transformation had been sublime but there could be not too much further to hope for an edifice that had had its actual foundations laid in the 13th century.

And I'll bet those cornerstones are even earlier.

Medieval, yes; Dark Ages – no.

A lot was going on then; the world was opening up, to Crusades, to voyages of trade, of conquest – to knowledge.

Thus had the 'Place House' come into being, first for the Abbotts whose determined collecting drew the attention of no one – and everyone with a plan. For here, amongst the tender ministrations of the White Canons, came a library the likes of which the then civilised world might envy – and how it had grown.

The Abbey was small – and poor – why then so many books?

For the books had come, from everywhere – theology, medicine, philosophy – and books of legends – all had found a place – here.

And centuries later, the ruins had taken on new life, rising again as the elegant home of the Earl of Southampton. A strong, wealthy and brilliant patron – and there, to Place House, had come, more likely than not – the gentle, passionate playwright from London – from Avon.

And the rest, as Abby might say – we baptised into history.

He did not stop to admire the work done to preserve Place House; his map directed him elsewhere and soon the ruins lay behind.

Yet not too far behind; for despite the allusions of the play, the seacoast itself might not be the target in question. What he sought was an access to water somewhat nearer, and one at least as mysterious as the story and setting of *The Tempest* itself.

He turned off the road – and there it was, stretching before him, overgrown, blazingly green – the New River – the Tichfield Canal.

The connection could not be missed – created by the Earls of Southampton – for purposes that still remained open to conjecture, subject to wild debate.

And what better way to secure a spot that might once have been both questionable – and potentially highly dangerous.

Plainly artificial; its origins are unknown, and it was clearly designed so that access was limited – no seaborne trade could enter here.

And for a very long time – at nearly the right time – it has lain between Tichfield – and the sea.

It took some time to get down there once he left the car.

He'd had far too little sleep, and his legs needed help. But he had good eyes and what he sought he soon found – half buried in the stones and scrub, a pinnacle or rounded capstone of dark rock loomed up.

Beneath it, concealed by the luxurious growth of years, was a doorway of some kind – and in fighting his way closer, he soon revealed a dank, half-choked tunnel entrance, small and dreadful.

Quist looked about. The area was deserted; the sky threatened rain or worse. Not a person watched him as he examined his find.

Briefly, but like a brick, it struck him that he truly didn't want to go into that dark doorway.

But scrambling with effort and hard digging out, with cane and hands – he had.

Now he made his way in – and very clearly down, glad that the pinnacle's roof was peppered with gaping holes. Some light came through, enough to keep him on his track, and not screaming, at a run, back out, away from this dreadful place.

For it was dreadful – tunnels, and underground corridors led off into the shadows, and the man who'd spent so much of his life in tunnels like these, digging underground was still overwhelmed.

It's the atmosphere – or rather the aura.

The air is clean enough, that argues for much.

There's just the rest of it, a sense of something foul, either in fact – or in some dark history – too long ago.

And these tunnels, they're everywhere – and I'll bet a great deal that many of them join, and interconnect.

And if the tides were right – a great many things other than books could be 'drowned' in here …

He marked his way as best he could, in hopes that wiser, more perceptive eyes could help him find the way back.

198

That is, if they can get here – for I've been certain all along that time runs against us in this, and those that follow us are as eager to kill, as to possess the prize.

He'd come to a branch point; long he considered – then the smell of the sea rose into his face, more strongly from one than the other – and he made his choice.

On, and down again; it soon became clear that seawater was close ahead, and a well, or pit of seawater was what he sought.

Fifty paces more and he regretted his choice.

Without warning, the sand and stony path seemed to tremble beneath his feet. A sizeable chunk of rock freed itself from the ceiling high above and plummeted down. It careened off the walls, landing finally with a heart-stopping crash right before him.

'Be not afeared, the Isle is full of noises!'

'Corragio!'

He pulled his whiskey flask from his jacket and took a hefty dose of courage, then pushed his way through a tight doorway in the rocks. After a mental vow to avoid lemon tarts, he got through and suddenly came out into a chamber.

A large room stretched before him

The walls were stone; strangely did it appear they had actually been pieced together. Heavily brined, they had been patched, and seaweed still laced within their crevices.

So well worked; it more than suggested they bore the marks of the hand of man.

Dried seaweed crunched underfoot and lay scattered on the floor of the chamber as he stepped forward; more tunnels went off into the dark but, there, in the very centre – lay a large well, or chasm, ringed by large black stones – and the sound of moving water rose to his ears.

Quist, the lover of mystery, ventured to the lip of the well. Within, the water rippled, its diminutive waves clearly roused by the tug of the sea, and here, the air seemed fresher and almost bracing.

But his determined inspection left him in no doubt.

There was nothing in the well but water, nothing that he could see; he had taken the wrong turn.

He turned his attention to the walls and there, under his hands came revelation.

This chamber is indeed not entirely natural.
For here are pictures – and words from a distant age.

The age of the symbols scattered across the wall could not be determined; at one point, Quist decided they had their origin from some date before the long millennium turned, back near the time of Christ. In the next moment, he thought he had under his hands a word that could be Old English.

Old Anglo Saxon? But strange, queer and corrupt, I just can't make it out.

Dearly did he wish he had his phone, for a photo now would be priceless.

The words were an enigma; the images drawn roughly across the stone proved even more mysterious – and soon much more ominous.

There painted across the rock in some unknown but apparently indelible stain were pictures – and one made the Professor draw away, with his breath caught in his throat.

Now I am in awe; now I am afraid – again.

Before my eyes – there is what cannot be other than a man – he wears a long cloak, he carries a staff – and there, at his feet – is a book.

And there, far in the distance – is that a dragon – or some such fabulous beast?

But it was the figure that stood just behind the cloaked man that gave Quist a shudder.

Tall it was; the outlines had been coarsely but deliberately filled to black opacity. This figure stood in flowing dark robes – regal – threatening – and its arm was stretched forth – in command.

He did not need to see a crown, there on the head of this etched apparition.

So; there You are at last. Regal, yes; queenly would be more to the point. And here You are, in a place where Power has lived loud, has lain buried for a long, long time.

He peered closer.

And who or what is that standing just behind You? And what is that upon the ground?

201

He stepped back; more dried algae crumbled under his boots. Bits of ancient leaves and dust rustled across the ground, hurried by a strange low breeze.

That wind was heavy with the scent of the sea, briny, bracing …

Yet vaguely hideous.

Something foul; worse than the odour of long-dead, dried fish – rotten – and strong.

He looked around the chamber again; now the walls seemed too close, ready to close about him, and fearing he knew not what – he hungered to escape, to find the safety of light, of the open air to leave this …

Cell.

It is exactly like a cell – and that word fills me with horror.

In sudden panic, he whirled about – for from deep within one of the darkest tunnels in the wall – a sound grew insistently louder – and the odour of corruption became a veritable miasma.

Undoubtedly, what shuffled now into view was the source of the frightful odour.

It was not a man, even less a likeness of one.

Dark, shrunken, its form bent low; the hairy arms twitched, moving restlessly as its blackened claws searched the ground – and the scholar recoiled in terror.

It is not human – this is some kind of half spirit, the poor wretched remains of what once walked a good deal more upright were it still fully alive.

Frightfully old was the thing that stood there and the human's mind was racing; into it came the story of *The Tempest* and one of its more deadly characters.

Was this the thing that stood for the original?
Is this terrible phantasm the hybrid creature Caliban?

Overcome by the rank scent and awful sight, Quist drew back – clouds must have passed overhead, blocking the pinnacle, for the chamber was grown dark, steeped in shadow. Now fearful of escape, Monty continued to back away, edging toward the tunnel that had brought him here – as the thing that once had held the moniker of 'monster' began to speak.

"I'll not fall flat for thee, as I did before – when thou didst bring me celestial liquor."

Inspiration struck the scholar, and he drew forth his flask again and held it up.

"This is all I have, and there's little in it."

What might once have been Caliban, eyed the flask and then the man. In the darkling light, its eyes glittered evilly as it marked the well-fleshed – and no longer youthful fellow in its cell – and Monty's heart raced as he readied himself for a desperate gamble.

"Share what thou hast – and mayhaps thou may leave timely before the tide rises," murmured the creature.

"Would you swear then to be my subject, Monster?"

The half-live thing glared at the man.

"I'll swear on nothing. This is my Isle – He got it from me by cunning, by *sorcery*."

"Thou liest."

It was not the wisest thing to say, for the unclean thing moved forward with alarming speed, and Quist backed away, making a swift and now terrified circuit around the well.

And here I am, in the bowels of the earth – with no weapons – no aid, and no mercy.

Here, helpless, and alone in the hungry dark.

For it was dark, and growing darker every moment, and Quist wondered how the sky could have grown so bereft, and shed its light so quickly.

Unless – that thing creates these shadows of itself – cursed, here in the dark.

This craven murderous thing makes the darkness now.

And pity moved him.

"Thou poor cursed soul …"

"Cursed; aye, cursed and left to rot in the dark. For Master went away long ago. And the tall Lady went with him. They quarreled, and Master lost. But, only for a time; the Lady's shade returned – and bade me wait. That Master would return, to people the earth – even as poor Caliban tried.

Ego vidi – I have seen!

Thunderstruck, paralyzed; Montgomery Quist froze where he stood.

Was a piece of the riddle now solved – unless this thing lies still, as before?

Darker grew the chamber, and the eyes of the thing of nightmare glowed out from the dark – and Quist despaired.

Help; help me, for I cannot see to run – and I have no weapon to fight this thing …

And it came …

What hast thou brought with thee, Wise Fool?

And the terrified man halted.

"Yes. Yes, thank you."

Quist stared down in the gloom, at the flask in his hand. Then he pulled from his pocket the cigarette lighter – one of the last things that had come to mind in a room far away – a thing no steadfast pipe man would deign to use – except for now.

And the man prayed with all his heart to Everything that came to mind now.

"I warn thee, Monster – let me pass."

"Nay," growled the thing. "Stay awhile – 'tis time to sup."

"Then – *come.*"

The Monster leapt at the man.

Quist stumbled back, feeling his feet slip on the sere, withered weeds, desperate now, for if all failed, here in this terrible place, away from the light and air – his life would be over.

With a last mighty effort, he scrambled back, away – and hoisted himself up – and took a mightier draft of the whiskey.

With a full mouthful of spirits, he extended his arm – and spat a thick spray of droplet laden vapour – directly at his attacker – and his finger raked across the lighter's spark wheel.

Now he fell back again, amazed.

Spirits do not light like that – without the aid of Spirit.

It was true; from the very heart of the cloud of burning vapour – a dazzling flame erupted. It reached up and about, igniting the dried tinder of withered leaf and weed – and engulfing Caliban.

Blinded by brilliance, the base creature howled as its form seethed with flame, star-like, unreal – impossible.

And before Quist's eyes, the body that the obscene spirit wore shattered – like air frozen into ice. Beneath that part falling away, the emaciated body of the being immortalised in verse shrieked, stumbled – and began to crawl – reaching for the well.

Montgomery Quist took to his heels and ran.

He ran, fleeing the distant howls of anguish, of defeat – until finally, at the last, there came the weak report of a body – striking hard into deep, deep water, to echo dimly in his ears.

CHAPTER 21

PEN AND SWORD

The man who had trained dozens of fighters – of warriors, in the decades of his career found himself in a place he had never expected to be.

Percy Onslow was on his knees in a sea of trampled grass.

There was blood there as well, mixed in with the cold dew of early morning. His jeans were wet through and the air misted before him with each painful, laboured breath.

But he had managed, with teeth and cursing and some dexterity, to get the tourniquet around his left arm.

Left. Right; no matter, I can fight as well with either. Assuming I see the dusk …

And the sword thrust missed all vital organs; except those of my pride – and my faith.

So quickly had he and Pen packed and left that there had been no time. He was certain; she had paid only the least attention to what he had tossed onto the back seat of the jeep.

She had seen such packs before; they inevitably held weapons and such, so she didn't raise a brow. She herself was beaming, enthused, thrilled

209

even to be finally on the way, on the hunt; her own bag had gone onto the car floor before her feet.

There had been room enough – if not enough time.

There could have been no way that Pen might have guessed what lay concealed in the pack her uncle had arranged, or what he bore close to his heart under his jacket.

Of that, he had been sure.

It had never occurred to him to ask the right question.

If she herself was armed.

The traffic was nonexistent; odd for the day and the season. The sun was full up by the time they had traversed an hour's worth of road – always west – always toward the coast.

But this sun, with its high cloud, its halo – for there was ice up there, quite high, was less than encouraging. In no time, they had hit a light rain, soon replaced by a sombre gray that wore away at the heart – that stood firmly in the way of clarity.

He had glanced upward as they sped along; there was the halo and the man's thoughts ran ahead.

A circle round the sun.

Behind the wheel or not, despite weather, isolation – I should have seen it coming.

He had slowed for the weather, or perhaps what came from some infernal machination, but out of nowhere, totally unexpected – it had come.

There ahead – the prone form of a body smack in their path, in the road.

Dark, motionless, it stretched across the way – and even in the scant sun, a glint came from the edge of the prone one's dark, voluminous coat.

Percy had brought the vehicle to a crawl. Pen's eyes were riveted; her whole body seemed rigid with – with what, he should by all rights have asked.

But he did not and it was his niece who spoke.

"Stop, Percy – we must stop."

Something in that voice, a voice that had been always recognisable – and now was not.

He frowned in sudden alarm; all his instincts, those instincts he tried so hard to awaken in his students were aroused, and real fear struck him like a hammer.

He glanced at the girl beside him – and her calm was unnerving. This was not like Pen, not like anyone who might just have seen a body in the roadway.

"No. We're going around," he said.

The girl's voice was low and terrifying.

"No. We're not."

And she reached across – and seized the wheel.

The jeep had nearly no forward momentum but with growing panic, Onslow fought her for the wheel as she pivoted – and her fist went into the side of his head.

He lost his hold; stunned, he felt the car swerve violently as she jerked the wheel hard and drove them up onto the parkway, hurtling across the sea of wet grass.

They careened to a halt; Pen yanked the keys from the jeep.

She grabbed her pack and was out of the car in a flash, running hard along the road and to his horror, he saw that the body had vanished – and the one he had treasured almost as his nearest kin – had dropped his keys on the pavement, and turned to face him – with a sword in her hand.

At moments like these, there is no time to question, either motive or intent – or even kinship.

His reactions were not those of an uncle, nearly a parent to the young woman in the road. He knew what he carried, he now suspected the goal of the ambush – he reacted as a warrior.

Onslow flung down the passenger seat, and from his own pack, he drew a sword – it was Fitzalan's blade – the Sorcerer's blade – and he left the jeep – and walked to meet the one he fervently hoped was mad.

For if she is – I may be able to overcome her.
If not, she is with the enemy – and I shall kill her.

There lay the measure of four long sword lengths between them when he came to a halt.

His eyes went over her; to the blade which must have been hidden by the jacket of the one in the road – the bait.

"Stand down," he said.

"No, uncle. You see – I can't. You have what I need. Put it on the road – and go. Just walk away."

The sun shone down with its ring of ice – a circle of light eerie, ghastly – and the thin pall of darkness, both real and supernatural fell across the two holding razor sharp blades in their hands.

And sent into lurid shadows the face of the one who stood with murder in her heart.

"Don't make me kill you, Pen," he said.

"You won't get the chance."

And she flew at him, her sword moving in an arc of glittering silver, as he met her furious attack stroke for stroke.

Pen was relentless; the girl had speed – the man strength. But the battle was unequal – for although Percy fought with all the savagery of need, of desperate mission – he also fought against the obvious need to kill this girl.

Thus it was her weapon that found its hits – arm, shoulder, across the face – and she remained relatively unscathed – for Percy Onslow would not kill her.

Onto the wet grass and down he went, rolling to one side and leaping up – nearly spent – and she came at him again.

213

And behind her, some distance away on the grass, Percy finally saw the means and the motive – the one who moved the pieces.

There stood Tam, in his sweeping black coat; he watched the fight calmly, callously – and the young Wizard's eyes were brilliant amidst the gray of cloud, of mist – of desperation on the field.

Finally, Pen drove Percy back, hard enough to make him stumble – to a standstill. He stood before her, bloody, clinging to consciousness – his chest heaved and his sword shook with each hard won breath.

And still he would not submit – as the girl stepped forward, with the point of her blade aimed at the man's eyes – and she cried out, in rage – in anguish.

"Leave it, Percy!"

And finding a strength deep within, unremitting and incomprehensible – he stiffened, and his back straightened and he stood upright again.

"No," he gasped.

"For the last time – throw it down!"

"*You go to Hell*," the sword master growled.

And the voice of the seducer came low and harsh.

"Kill him," said the Wizard. "He'll kill you if you don't – *kill him*."

And Tam drew nearer and greed and lust and bloodlust lit his face.

And anguish was on her face as she beheld Percy Onslow, conquered but unfallen.

And she saw the man who had been there – helping her grow – learn – and live – and the thought of him lying at her feet, with the insurmountable barrier of death between them drew a terrible cry from the girl.

Before he could parry, she leapt forward and slammed the hilt of her sword across his face.

Thunder sounded above, and the swordsman went down in a heap onto the turf made slick with blood.

He was only dimly aware, as she ran to him, searched his jacket, and stepped away – with the fragment of the Star Taker in her hand.

A thin stream of blood ran down the length of Pen's sword – and now lightning flashed, cutting the sky directly above them in a blinding arc – as the wind came to life, as the rush became a roar – and within that roar, as the world darkened – there came a *Voice* – one fell, hellish, apocalyptic and infinitely menacing.

Leave him.

Terror closed in, and in an agony of shame and fright, Pen picked up her pack and raced away – and Tam followed after.

Onslow fought the pain and nausea of her blow, watching with bleared eyes as the two vanished down the road, then left it for the darkness under the trees.

For it was dark – and not just beneath the trees. Clouds foamed overhead; the dreadful croak of distant ravens came to the man on the ground.

He was utterly alone.

For a moment, the wounded one wished for mercy, for the stroke of the next bolt overhead – such was his loss, such was his sorrow and despair.

Both.

The Star Taker.

And my faith.

Pen. Both gone.

His head bowed.

And the wind died – soft across his bloody face, fingers of light rain, cool and gentle, fell.

Bracing was the mist that curled across his brow, his pale but burning cheeks.

And the broken man's blood fell in drops, passing through the grass so close to his head, into the arms of the waiting and watching earth – and a murmur came up from deep below and in silence, his head lowered to the ground.

He had only been out for a few seconds.

Now he started back to life, and the swordsman shivered on the grass, as, with a mighty and agonising effort, he nearly raised himself onto his knees.

He was wounded and in despair; for many moments it took all Percy Onslow had just to hold off collapse.

Failure; in body and spirit.

And in purpose; for with that piece of the Taker, Tam has the means to raise the Book, open it – and open the Gate.

He lacks but one piece more – and the secret of the Key – then we have lost all.

I failed.

His head bowed again; tears filled the warrior's eyes – for betrayal had come – and he had not forestalled it – and it would cost them all dear.

Cost everything, everything I thought sure – my family, my life, it would seem.

Without hope, he knelt in the cold grass and a shaking hand raised to his face came away with bright blood.

"Wilt thou surrender this easily, mortal?"

Rigid with fear, weakened by combat and despair, the sword master started violently and his hand went down to steady himself.

The Voice was indescribable; it had come from the shadows under the tall trees that skirted this narrow meadow of grass beside the roadway.

Within that shadow came the gleam of eyes – dazed, but tenacious, Percy hauled himself upright and raised the only remaining true weapon he had left

– his sword – for his spirit was still gripped by horror and sorrow.

A moment later, the wounded man backed unsteadily away, then fell heavily back onto his knees.

For a figure had stepped forward from the shelter of the trees, and the sight of this One was spellbinding and dreadful beyond words.

Impossible to describe verily, even for one who had seen such marvels that would have left abashed the faculties of the common man.

Like a man – yet It is not.

A form made of shifting silver, light and flickering shadows – all made flesh. The hair – full and flowing, lifting and swirling by some breath of Spirit – a Being of smoke made solid – of fire that burns, yet does not consume.

Here is a denizen of the space 'between' – between what we call our world – and the worlds that actually exist, unseen yet mighty – just beyond our grasp.

Here is power – the likes of which I have never seen – never imagined – but then, I did not know Solomon …

He had guessed rightly.

For an artless semblance of a smile cross the Spirit's face – and Percy's voice quavered.

"Your name …"

"Thou hast no need to know. Put aside thy blade."

Hurriedly, Onslow placed the sword on the ground.

"Ah! Iron … ," he said.

"Nay. I shall send it after. In that which is thy weapon – and clearly I see the skill, the mastery with which it has been wrought – there is much steel – it may hinder us."

"Us?"

And the man's mind raced.

How is this Thing here? Who sent It?

It would take a will even Caspian Hythe does not yet have – a mastery of power. Ah … Yes.

The Djinn drew near, then to Onslow's horror It sat cross-legged on the turf directly before him.

He froze where he was – for the Being was studying him closely – his hands, his shoulders – the many scars on the bared arms – the face where, once, a young man's stroke had gone amiss – or had struck perilously true.

The eyes of the Djinn narrowed; the Spirit looked deeply into him and Percy Onslow had a sight he would take to his grave – for within the eyes of the demon, the One Hidden From Sight – colour had somehow joined with Spirit.

Fire – and smoke – both there, circling there about a pupil whose darkness is merely a window, into a place where humankind can never enter.

The eyes of the demon are of all the worlds – of paradise, of the afterlife – the endless realms of torment and delight.

And Percy spoke, and the intent of his words came from his heart, without thought.

"How can I serve Thee?"

Fire flashed in the Djinn's wondrous eyes and what could only be described as a look of deference came to Its face.

"Mortal – do not trust too readily. It is Our place to serve Thee – and always at a price. What wouldst thou now? Thou art a warrior; wouldst thou go forward, take the appointed path – perhaps to die? Or languish here, alive – in defeat – though none should know of it."

The man took a painful breath.

"I'm wounded. I …I'm afraid."

The demon was silent; the immortal closely watched the mortal.

Percy said nothing – and the scent of the man's blood came full into the demon's face.

"If Thou walk the harder path – I may heal – only thy courage. And I may guarantee only the prospect of battle well fought – and if it comes – a rest untainted by shame, untroubled by remorse."

"None of my kind have ever asked for — or expected any more. It is enough."

The demon smiled and rose, to stand towering over the man.

And the Djinn reached down, extending a glowing hand and with his heart in his mouth, Percy Onslow reached up and the man's fingers interlaced with those of the demon – at whose tips, razor sharp talons lay.

Like a lightning bolt, an agonizing pain, sharp and cold as ice shot upward from the man's hand. As cold as ice, as if fire and ice were one, the claws of unbearable pain climbed up the helpless man. By the time they had reached his heart, he felt gripped by an icy cold, so relentless and pitiless, he felt his heart must choke with it.

Like frigid poison, the cold knotted itself in his veins as blue fire curled about the man and the demon. Deafened by the maelstrom's roar, with his eyes blinded by the light that billowed over them, the swordsman collapsed.

His scream was lost to his ears, as his mind lost all sensibility.

Had anyone been there, they might have seen a wondrous thing – as a fallen man, there upon the grass became one with a strange smoke and living cloud – how he was there one moment, and in the next was gone.

The man and the Djinn had vanished.

Then, ghostlike on the trampled grass – the outlines of Caspian Hythe's sword grew dim.

The bright steel wavered, becoming nearly transparent – and deep within the outline of the blade, a bright point of light appeared.

Even as the iron and steel were made and unmade, even as they began to fade from sight – light

221

and shadow warred about the *symbol* that had lain buried, deep within the weapon.

A moment later, that sign grew blinding – and the sword itself blazed brilliantly – and the symbol rested clear and prominent on the blade of the Sorcerer – the sword girt with the runes and hearts of legend.

Then all faded.

In a heartbeat, there was only the sound of the birds. There was only the wet grass, bent and bloody, left to greet the rising sun's rays.

CHAPTER 22

POWER IS

I hate this part; always have – always will.

He had risen to his feet a little too quickly; now Cass took great heaving breaths, trying to force down the nausea, arrest the vertigo.

Not the time for unsteady legs – unsteady will.

Even with the Gnome's help, the passage through the Gate at the church grounds had claimed its usual dues – both the Knight and the Mage had come to their senses, dizzy, disoriented, and on the ground, near to the woods that bordered this expanse of meadow – of antiquity.

There within sight were the ruins of the Abbey that was before – with its library, with its infernal link to a monstrous Book. And the ruins of Place House – so modern in comparison.

And time was running out.

Unknown was how this exact destination had been processed by the Gnome.

The Sorcerer could only guess how, unfathomable as to time and means – at the very edge of these woods, a portal had been established.

Just how had been the question from the first, for all the Gates.

Long ago, Quist, ever the scholar, ever the inquisitive mind had enquired after the origins of this kind of travel, and had in the mildest tones, enquired directly about the Gates.

It was of course the give-away; when Monty tossed off a question, there was always a grenade tied to it.

"How does it work, old fellow? I don't mean the actual dynamics – who hasn't played with the idea of gates and portals? Just live stream the latest flick on your device of choice."

But the Gates themselves – their location – that was what lay at the utterly unmurky bottom of Quist's mind.

And always Cass' as well.

For he had had no clear answer as to how or where the location of destinations had been devised, and very clearly constructed.

Or by whom.

The Sorcerer had proclaimed rightful ignorance; it was true in only the most superficial sense – and the question had gone to sleep again.

Too much needed now – far too fast, to give this the thought it deserved. But the Mage had his suspicions, deep ones and he guessed Monty had begun to ride in on the same horse.

At the moment, he and the Knight rested where they lay, stiff and cold from the passage. And

Ava had stared and pointed, back – to a spot somewhere under the tall trees nearly overhead.

"There – we came through in there."

As with loud cries, ravens broke from the cover of those trees and their wings were dark across the sky, against the clouds that hung heavy with moisture, scudding in from the sea.

They were indeed close to the sea; again came the tang of salt laden air – and Cass breathed deep the incense of moving water, the vivid air of seaweeds cast along a shore, along a sandy, stone strewn shore.

And a vision of a deep, dimly lit chamber, with light flickering down through castle-like fenestrations in a stone ceiling came to him …

They were close, indeed.

For the Abbey was close, indeed.

Tall, still imposing, two towers soared, remaining at the very front of the battered edifice. They climbed upward, glowering down, in seemingly imperishable solidity. Their stern gaze was over the wide meadow of a modern site, one still actively studied and under excavation.

For what lay beneath the bricks of Place House was still a mystery – and to the Mage came a strange sense that what was left, sleeping below was still a powerful baffling, a shield – still alive – still vigilant.

225

When he looked over, he saw that the Knight had risen; now she stood silent, gazing at the rear of the building, all broken, all imponderable.

"Something – there's still something in the air, in the ground below the Renaissance ruin. That house is old, Cass – and what lies beneath the foundations – beneath the lost Abbey – that goes back even further."

Dark were the wings still soaring across the sky; the ravens circled overhead and their cries, harsh and croaking floated down to the two standing below.

They walked stiffly to the front, then passed through the doors – and rain spattered down as they came into the furthest side of the wide courtyard. Here, open to the sky now, once had lain the library of the Canons. Then time passed – a house had been built over the ruins of that eldest place – erected here, only to fall in its turn, into the ruins where they stood now.

The two looked about; scattered across the courtyard and beyond, history lay untapped – at least for the two seeking the signs. Tiles and bricks, broken and incomplete but many marked with exotic designs spread before them.

And the Mage looked about, for something about the place seemed familiar – and the words came back to his mind.

The course that goes around the sun …

And he began to walk, moving to the centre of the courtyard, walking back and forth – and Ava called out to him.

"Here."

She stood not far away – there, half-buried in the turf and sand – lay a flat tile – with the image of a sun graven across its cold surface.

He strode away, searching for the course in the rhyme – and there it came.

A rough path did indeed reach round the sun – it was in the bits and pieces of the stones and tiles that littered the site – and they made a rough circuit about the central image of a rayed sun on an old stone.

Around once – the Knight followed after; both peered side to side.

Around again – and something seemed to shift – and the Sorcerer looked back at the way they had come and turned to the Knight.

"Was that stone there before?"

She stared.

"Not possible – they can't be moving, can they?"

"We both just went through something close to the centre of the earth – how can you honestly be asking that?"

Back they went, around again, until weary and desperate they halted.

"The Gnome – he spoke of an urn."

227

"I don't see one – not even one in pieces."

"Look again."

Round they went – and now Ava cried out – and crouched close to the ground.

From the distance came again the cries of ravens; the clouds had returned, rain threatened – and curiously chill grew the air.

And Cass looked about, for the sense of something impending, something looming imminently was overwhelming.

He took out his dagger, and knelt beside her.

Below them, nearly hidden in the deep grass and covered with the leaves and twigs that the winds of many winters had lifted and scattered – there peeped out an edge of tile.

Along its border – a line of curling vine – or bracken.

Both set to work; Cass' dagger loosened the turf, and Ava's long fingers went over the tile, removing, loosening until the litter of the ages was gently swept aside – and her fingers went under the edge of the flat ceramic – a tile, and across its surface, the image of an urn, battered and broken.

With infinite care, she lifted the tile.

Root and rock below – these Cass cleared until his fingers met something hard.

Another tile lay buried deep; like the first, this one had symbols upon it, and its surface glinted in the dim light.

228

"It's almost forged – as if someone had taken stone and cast it in iron or bronze."

This stone the Mage lifted to reveal a small cavity, clearly man – made.

And within, protected from time and elements and the hand of man – lay a sheet of folded parchment, one ancient and intact. It did not quite cover that which lay beneath – that gleamed like newly minted gold or bronze.

Both on their knees; both stunned.

For the parchment was inscribed and the words in legible but archaic tongue – were terrible.

> *Who finds Me here,*
> *Must walk in fear.*
> *For then the end of*
> *Men is near.*
> *But hold ye fast, the final*
> *Key. In blood –shall*
> *Closed or open Be.*

And from within the parchment, a folded bit of something fluttered down.

It was a page of some kind; laden with words and symbols.

Like the page of a book.

There within the little crypt lay something else, dark – it was a key. It went into Cass' hand, and with the folded page, both went into his pocket.

Their search was over.

Ava reached down and took into her hand the last piece of the Star Taker. She turned it over and gasped; there on the back, graven along the edge of the bright metal itself, was part of a map, the same direction as that which had led Monty to the door hidden at a strange pinnacle of rock.

"See! It's just there, just across the way! We've got to get out of here!"

"Not so fast," came the dark reply from across the courtyard.

The two leapt up; there, at the entrance to the site stood Tam, sword in hand – with her dagger drawn, Pen stood with him.

There was no time for shock.

"Thank you, brother – for finding it so quickly."

And the young Wizard held out his hand.

"I'm not your damned brother," snarled Cass – and with dagger raised, he hurled himself at Tam.

Impossible – unequal – the prowess of the Mage was no match – he could not withstand the power, the savagery of the one with the sword – for Tam was equally desperate, and the passage through the Gate still sapped the Sorcerer's strength.

Blow after blow rained down on the Mage, and he was driven back – the Knight fared little better. Her dagger went blade to blade with Pen's, even the Star Taker served for she wielded it as a main-gauche.

To no avail. Pen forced the Knight backward then onto her knees – and Cass bled freely from cuts across his arms and face.

In a flash, Pen's boot went into Ava's face – and the girl yanked the Taker from her grip. Cass was also down; Tam stood over him, with the point of his sword at Cass' throat.

Pen tossed the Taker to her partner; the young assassin hovered over the two on the ground and with his eyes gleaming, his gaze went over the relic.

"It's time for us to go," said Tam. "But I cannot leave without some token – let us see what we can give you – for enjoyment – for challenge. But follow, Cass – *follow*."

Terrible words; enigmatic if only for the moment.

For the young man stepped away – his next words floated on the air, lost in the breeze – then he and the kin of Percy Onslow backed away, and vanished through the doorway of the site.

The Knight and the Mage were silent; their heads lowered in shame, in dismay – for the Taker was gone, and the enemy had flown.

All was lost.

Then terror came; the two on the ground watched, as clouds mounted even higher, darker still, directly overhead – and an uncanny darkness lowered over the ruins.

And rain flooded down – rain, from clouds that before had held only a breath of moisture – water soon pooled about the entire meadow, water deepened everywhere, until the Mage and the Knight struggled against their wounds to stand, to keep their heads afloat.

Their heads were not the only ones in danger of the rain – for from all throughout the ruins, rats had begun to race.

"Rats?" gasped the Mage.

"If only …"

For, desperate to escape the flood – and with each moment – those rats began to change.

There were not many – but in several moments, each had grown to massive size, and as the rain slowed, the two humans watched in horror as those aberrant things caught sight of them – and began to scurry forward.

Cass and Ava pulled themselves upright, backed away; their weapons were all they had.

"She did it once. How did Alice escape the sea of tears?" he cried.

"She swam away – and the mouse went with her."

"Not an option here," said Cass, as the first of the rodents, as large as a small dog made a leap for his throat.

232

He struggled with the demon beast as Ava's dagger went across the hides of two more.

"He raised these from flesh – into spirit! But they're just alive enough to kill us!"

Daggers out, they backed while the corporal, bestial incarnations of once gentle rodents advanced upon them.

Two sprang; the Knight's long dagger slashed the throat of one, and she slammed the other to the ground. More scurried forward and the Mage had his own blade soon red with blood as dark claws scrabbled forward, the livid paws working in the slick grass.

Those hellish beasts that fell writhed, died, and struggled – to *rise* again, and in desperation, Ava fought her way to the Sorcerer's side.

"They are *half spirit*," she cried.

And reaching into the sac that Onslow had given to her, that had traveled with her since they had left Abby's bed – she pulled forth the Orb, and held it out to the Mage.

And weary unto death, pale from his wounds, the Sorcerer fought to remain standing, to overcome, and the words of the Gryphon came to him again.

Give all.

Now as stormy, as grey and dark as the thick clouds – the eyes of Caspian Hythe fixed upon the tall imposing ramparts of a finer age.

And Cass took the sphere and raised his dagger – and Ava watched as time slowed, and faltered in its relentless track.

From the heart of the storm, lightning flashed – yet it etched a leisurely bolt against the sky, and the sound of thunder was quenched, its roar arrested by some mystifying force, unable to build.

And when she turned to her companion, she stood transfixed.

The modern clothes of the man she knew were fading. Before her eyes, the very fabric of his form was shifting.

The one before her now bore resemblance to the Mage, but that was all.

Shadow masked, the man at her side was garbed in leather; a jerkin and the breeches of another age covered the chest and limbs of the Sorcerer.

He still held the Orb – it blazed now in a hand whose arm was clad in gauntlets – the dagger he had held was now a broadsword, bright but ancient, one whose fuller swam with fresh blood.

And that Orb had grown; massive and glowing brightly, the Eye of the First Gryphon hung in the air above the hand of the one at her side and the Orb's surface blazed like fire, bearing the maps of the heavens, and stars ranged in restless movement across the surface of the Orb.

And the Sorcerer's face was suffused with light.

Ava could not hear the words he spoke – but the dim outlines of the Abbey's ruins began a breathtaking transformation.

Stone by stone, each was etched in sapphire.

Blue light billowed across each and every brick of the hallowed place, and the structure, enduring and mighty still, was bathed in eerie light.

The monstrous creatures stood rapt – frozen in a mass before the towers, before the ruins of a house whose foundations lay deep – hallowed, whose roots preceded our age by somewhat less than a millennium.

Power spoke to power.

And the voice of the Mage rang out, guttural and deep – and the Voice of the Earth bellowed back in answer.

From beneath their feet – from below the spirit-edifice before them came a rumble, of horrifying, indomitable power – and the earth heaved up, rearing upward until the bright glow of the Abbey was shaken in its grip – and stone by stone, the spirit-ruins began to tremble – and fall.

Ramparts shuddered, as whole sections of the face shook, tottered, and plummeted.

And the mortals drew back, scrambling away as the crumbling walls fell, and buried the hordes of hellish things that Tam had reared into new and unnatural life.

The spectre of supernatural dust rose from the debris scattered across the meadow, where water had ceased to flow, where the floods had been staunched.

There was no sign of any living Hell beasts.

There was no sign of any life at all.

The forms of those creatures that had escaped the tumult began to change – frigid smoke curled luminously about them until they were utterly obscured – and when the pale, cold mists parted, rising to vanish with the breeze, the bodies of the demon things were gone as well.

Then haltingly but purposefully – the fallen ramparts of the House – the Abbey – began to move. Brick by brick, in mortar and wood – all aglow with sapphire – each rose to recover its place in the whole.

In moments, the spirit- edifice was restored.

In moments more, the halo of blue light evaporated – and the actual ruins stood as they had always been.

Torn and scattered like the shreds of old dreams, the darkness lifted away; the air was clear and light, pure and fresh.

The startling and baffling garb of the Mage had also vanished.

Now back in his proper clothes, drained in body and spirit, with a thin trickle of fresh blood at his nostrils – Caspian Hythe slid to his knees – and the Knight rushed to his side.

CHAPTER 23

THREE ARE TESTED

Slowly He made his way down, and forward, in the very tracks of the man He himself would have most aptly described as the *Scholar*.

Had Quist known, he would have felt the high honour.

Like the one who had traversed this tunnel before Him, the Master walked alone.

The way was not strange to Him, or frightening, as it had been to Montgomery Quist; it had been a very long time since His boots had crossed over these stones, this sand.

But He knew the way.

The land had changed above since His last sojourn here. Forests had fallen; low trees, houses, and the general clutter associated with the word 'humanity' had taken the place of the open fields, hedgerows, and mighty trees that He had known before.

The coast had changed; sandbars had moved, the little spits of sand that seemed so like *islands* before had moved, and some had vanished, washed away by the tides of centuries and the ever busy hands of men.

The accents of those living by those shores had changed, as had their dress.

Yet men are men; they do not change with the necessity of need, not nearly fast enough.

And they do not change at all – unless terrible things occur, unless they are threatened in the moment – for, as are the Wise, they are proof against their own folly.

And He recalled how the Wise had been tried before – and failed – and a great scourge now lay waiting – for the right hand.

Once more.

We failed; and now the Thing threatens to rise again, to conquer if it can – and again, the tests of the hearts of men, and of the Wise – will make the difference.

And I pray, this time – we shall all pass the tests.

Down He went, as Others had gone, down until the scent of water, of seawater fresh and moving, came again to His nostrils – and this time, those nostrils, that face, as well as the hand that rose to wipe away the precious sweat – all were those of a living man.

And He relished this form, these moments that He had known before, and lost, by his own folly – through the folly of arrogance, of misplaced trust, of power used unwisely.

He wended His way, passing stony corridors, until He had come to a split in the path; here He paused for He had been bidden to halt, to wait – and knowing the danger, ready for the deception, He had halted.

For one of the last tests.

And the dark stone and rock walls around him *changed*, and colours shifted and streamed – sending light over Him, around Him – and from one pale wall – the Voice came.

"Welcome – Brother."

"What do You want."

"I want the end – of strife, of that past, that *loss* on which both our thoughts dwell. For the seeds sown long ago have borne strange fruit, and more is to come."

The Master's eyes grew brilliant.

"What do You want."

The Voice altered; now it would have sweetened its tone if it could.

"I want what You stole from Me; what is rightfully Mine. It comes – with Your aid – or with Your life. Come to Me. Share it with Me."

A terrible moment, as doubt crossed the face of the Master, as He fought against the memory of an ancient tie, an unforgiveable bond.

And the moment passed.

"*You* – who never bestow – *anything* – except misery, and death, now offer to 'share'? I see You wear a different guise, but it confounds no one. And Your words are the same as before, lies and false

239

promise. *No – I will not aid You – and You are not my Brother."*

The mask dropped; the cloak fell.

The dulcet tones changed to a low, guttural snarl. Savage and ageless, resonant with malice, terrifying to any but the One who stood here – the Voice echoed like a growl in the cavern.

"There is just enough of Him left – for what is needed."

The Master stepped back – as far behind, the walls of the cavern shook, split and began to fall.

A rain of dust and shards of rock filled the air – as the cavern before the One now shook as well.

He was caught.

Trapped between falling walls and the heaps of boulders and stones that swiftly choked the passage, before and behind, He stumbled.

The sound of burial, of rending and catapulting stone ceased; all fell into silence.

The colours floating in the wall shifted and faded away; when the dust cleared, the man was nowhere in sight – and the path was barred.

I thought I knew; I didn't – for just one level down – and here we find Hell.

Thus it happened that the scholar, the man who loved a mystery stood confronted by it – and it seemed likely to cost him his life.

And I truly hope that it costs no one else's – for that, to ensure that end, not so gladly would I give my own.

He stood now in the place of Doom – no exaggeration, for Quist saw clearly what this place was – what it signified, the price – the cost of what this Thing might bring to the world.

And those that know of it – my friends, indeed, my family – what cost to them, for they are on the front line of the resistance.

If they arrive in time.

And here am I – the oldest, the weakest, without sword or wand or even flask.

He took a deep breath; then stepped from the high cavern corridor hewn from the cold rock, and walked toward the well in the centre of the chamber.

He knew this place; there were the stony walls that soared high, there the many openings, like doors in the chamber itself. He only hoped that the prior vision, taken from that infernal Orb had not designated him as the weak link – the one who might bring all down in chaos.

Terrible – if that is why I have been spared, for it suggests that all that has happened, all that has happened to me, that I have survived – was driven and directed by dark forces – rather than those of light.

His shoulders squared – and he walked over the sand and dark stone floor, as light filtered down from above, in quite the same way as it had in his mind, as his boots rustled through the thin piles of dry seaweed and shells – until he stood near the lip of the Abyss.

Suddenly the scent of the sea, the scent of flowers, of green growth came to him and the dark water just below the lip rippled as he drew nearer.

It is the scent of paradise – for those too unwise, too weak, too greedy to see – that this is a snare for the unwary – for those who would disguise and confuse their lust for the fantasy of doing good on a grand scale.

Those who would work miracles overnight, that properly take years and the spirits of many to achieve.

For only that is the path – to true wisdom, which has nothing to do with knowledge.

So it has always been, the need to cure with the speed of thought and no responsibility for what comes after.

Under his eyes, the water swirled.

A thin web of bright green algae curled, charting a lazy course across the restless water in the black pit; waves slapped gently against the dark rocks that lined the well and soothing and refreshing was their rhythm and that sound, as it always soothes, when man contemplates that rolling surf, hears that sweet melody of the living sea.

This was not true sea; the lulling tempo of the water was meant to lure – to draw near the awestruck, to reach the souls of the fragile – to draw them to what lay below the bright surface.

So was Montgomery Quist, weary, bruised and exhausted drawn; so it was that he peered down.

There, as in the vision, it lay, in all its ephemeral glory, in all its real threat.

Lovely, how beautiful.

It beckons – brighter and more golden than that damned apple.

At least the apple led us to some form of self-awareness – to some form of ability – even to some sense of shame for the ill-conceived too hasty act.

For it is shame, our own shame of ourselves – when we subvert our good for gain, when we willfully deny food, and air, and sustenance to body and soul – that we need to feel sometimes.

We should feel the shame of doing what we know is wrong – then we step back onto the real way.

So that apple did not fail us utterly.

For now, we cannot do other – than know.

There – on the narrow shelf coming out of the well wall – was an object of fear and loathing. It lay waiting; he saw the bindings, the lock – he observed the cover of the Book, with its fine leather untouched by time, by wave or wear.

Impossible; that it can look that way.

Yet it does – for it does not exist the way we think of existence, it does not survive in the sense we know as survival.

And yet it is alive – that, I can feel.

With an effort, for the desire to touch the thing was so strong – he pulled himself away.

A few deep breaths, and he began to search around him.

243

Several paces from the well he found one – a stone of good size and heft – for it came to this adventurer, bereft of wand or weapon, that some simple Neanderthal strength might dislodge the Book from its perch on that ledge.

And drive it deeper – buy us all some time – until the real artillery appears.

He hauled it up and turned.

"That won't do, old man."

Shock on that old man's face – he let the stone slip to the sand – and faced Pen, as she stood in the doorway to the chamber.

She came in and stood over the well; her eyes were bright but strange – the look in them as she studied the Book – gave a thrill of fear to the man on the far side of the well.

Then, she turned and walked away, back to the cavern door and faced him again.

"We both know that it will take more than one stone to settle this. We both know that you are too late – with stones, or anything else."

His heart sank; she should not be here, how could she be here, in this dreadful place – and calm beside that dreadful thing?

"I can only guess why you are here – and how."

"Can you."

He walked closer to her.

"Why, of course; I'm not completely dim. I saw the look in your eyes at that fateful meeting. I thought then it was the light of revelation – not the light I see now."

"And what is that."

"Of pure, simple greed. Of delusion, if you will. Oh, my dear, I do wish you had never come down from school. Not this time – not now."

For a second a terrible look crossed her face and her voice went to nearly a murmur.

"I do believe … my uncle wishes that, too. At least, I hope he still does."

Frank dismay was on Quist's face.

Dear God – what has she done?

And where is Percy Onslow?

Darkness fell over his heart as he spoke.

"Where is … your uncle?"

She turned in anger, in frustration.

"I mean to do this! I can do it – it's easy, Monty – why don't any of you see this?"

Now she paced, and her words came fast and furious.

"This is the thing that can save millions, solve everything."

"Whose everything, Pen? Do you trust the judgment of just one individual – to act for all?"

"No, but, …"

Now he drew closer, insistent, determined.

""Whom do you know – *right now* – that you could trust to make those choices – *right now?* I know, you can't really trust anyone to do that, and not because you are bad, or stupid or ignorant, or uncaring. The simple truth is that *no one is infallible*. No one will justly do what is best for all – unless the One walks the earth again, or perhaps the Wise gather together and ask the men and women of earth to come forward. Only then, if we pledge to follow what we call Divine Will, or rise to a level of thought that we have never attained before, might this work. Pen, this Thing – has been here for centuries. Before that, it wandered the earth like a pilgrim, not one of good, but one of hate, of terror – of uncontrollable Power."

"No, Monty – you're wrong!"

"*If it could have been done before, Pen – why has no one done it?* It cannot be unmade, it cannot be controlled – only hidden, and weakened, until we have the sense to turn away – and find those answers ourselves."

A great moment of silence followed – while Monty held his breath, and prayed.

But the girl turned back; her face was frightful and the one before him was a stranger to him.

"You are wrong. I am different from them, all of them – I have been from the very beginning."

His eyes narrowed.

"Those words – they do not come from *you* – *do they?*"

246

She paled – and raised up a dagger.

Intricate and beautiful were the hilts, of gold and silver – long was the blade, and finely wrought – and it glittered in the sudden surge of light – from the cursed well, billowing – where an ageless evil lay, camouflaged and false, waiting for the right hand, the final Key.

"What does their source matter? What matters is that I am no longer alone – as I see I have been all my life."

And the Professor made a last desperate plea, for he saw now the path of the villainy that had corrupted the girl, he saw how that seduction had played and delivered her into the enemy's hand.

"*You have never been alone – ever* – that is the lie that he fostered – in himself, I'll warrant – and now – in you."

Her eyes were like diamonds, unreal; her soul unreachable.

"I will build a better world; I'll take what is mine and use it. Let me pass, old man."

It was hopeless; with his strength waning, with no defense at all that he could see; it could finish no other way.

Perhaps this is where it all ends for me.
Here, in the dark.
Wait for me, Abigail.

Then he stepped before her, just paces away. Raising his cane, he leveled it and held it firm by each of its ends.

And in a white-knuckled grip – Montgomery Quist barred the way into the chamber.

"I will not."

There came a sudden shock – of stone moving, shifting – and from a great distance, the terrible echo of rock careening and falling – and Tam came up from behind the girl, and took his place beside her.

CHAPTER 24

THE TEMPEST

His words were light; his mood beyond grim.

"I seem to recall you advised expecting the unexpected."

The Knight's brows knit.

"I didn't actually mean this."

The Mage and the Knight stood side by side in the high, chiseled doorway of the chamber.

Not that much blood.

Not really.

He was wrong.

As the two had left the safety of the land, of the upper air, and descended, passing through the hidden door, a trail of small but bright spots of blood had marked their progress.

It had taken them much less than an hour to reach this level – this room, for room it must have been in some remote time.

As in another chamber not far away, where Quist had met horrific evidence of an actual origin to the Bard's lurid tale – these walls bore the marks of skilled hands – here, again, crude but purposeful illustration graced the otherwise dark chiseled surfaces.

He and Ava had pushed past the door in the rock pinnacle – and the Sorcerer had hesitated. The Knight had also halted; now she looked back at him.

Her wounds were not slight, nor were his – yet she wondered if the battle at the Abbey would prove their undoing.

He is weakened, but he is not weak.

Since that time before the dawn, from the house, to the ruins at the church – to the calling of the Gnome – I have watched this man grow, so rapidly, so fixedly and determinedly – that I can but wonder at the Gnome's warning.

Caspian Hythe is not weak.

He never has been.

Yet the months of doubt, of sorrow – of mourning – had taken their toll on the Mage. Ava had never seen him like this.

So reflective.

In all our time before, and 'Below', he was the one ready to charge ahead. What I see now is different.

He is not afraid.

He has grown.

Perceptive, appraising, quick but careful – reflective, wary of situation, careful of assumption.

What the Knight saw now was a seasoned, hardened fighter, a poised warrior, one who had passed through some dark tempering in a time, in a place she herself had missed.

Hell – it looks like he has been to Hell and back.

What had happened in that past – how had he come to doubt himself, to seek the training and discipline that would reconcile that event – with his need. What had Cass done there – or what had he not done?

For the man had changed; with some unknown core darker than before, yet was he canny, wiser, more the warrior than she had ever seen before in him.

Onslow.

This is Onslow's work – he had somehow known, guessed the need, apprised the desperate urgency for rapid action – he has honed Caspian Hythe as though he were sharpening a blade.

For what purpose?

There it lay before them, in a dark, hidden place – one disguised but not forgotten. There it waited – an open wound in the skin of space and time, a scar on the face of a frightened earth.

Here as everywhere, many corridors of stone opened upon this place; they were dark and shadowed.

The edges of the well in the centre of the chamber were only slightly raised above the stones that ringed the chasm. Dark seaweeds laced about their wet surfaces and hung dripping; shallow pools of seawater lay across a floor of sandy stone.

The ocean had not relinquished its hold on this unhallowed place – dimly, from a great distance,

251

came the bell-like tones of the sea, its waves broke close by, off the coast.

The pinnacle's roof extended over their heads; breached and channeled by the relentless hand of centuries, through the cracks light shimmered down. It was neither bright nor static but prismatic and a cascade of luminescence rendered the dark walls and floors into sharp clarity.

"It's uncanny," said the Knight. "It's horrible."

Then boldly did she leave the Mage, to venture closer to the pit. Cass came to her side – and she looked down.

The sides of the chasm were less finished than the chamber itself. Dark, eternally wet; fragmentary waves lapped restlessly and endlessly against the dark stone and the water was fresh and clear with the scent of the living sea.

Ledges protruded inward from the walls – and there – on one just below arm's length – something lay, and its outlines were indistinct with the mosaic of moving water.

"I see it, Cass."

And to the minds of both came words, sweet and dulcet – but cold and dead.

Touch Me and see Thou treasured lands,
I give Thee peace and fortune's hands.
Hear Thou my words,

252

Take Me this day. Find riches, joy;
The Golden way.

Below It lies …
A Gateway to the Shadowed skies.
And deep within the Toothéd Way,
The Doom of men, the blackest day.
Turn the Page, through Pages go,
Touch Thee this Thing –
Find endless woe.

The Sorcerer peered down. Less clear to his senses – less clear to his vision was the scene below.

"What do you see there, Ava."

Below, tendrils of seaweed, bright and lacy and green, swirled in the water and algae clustered with small shells clung to the well's walls.

On the narrow stony shelf lay the Book, and its chains and lock, heavy with verdigris, still shone.

Bright – enchanting – inviting.

A moment passed; the Knight's gaze narrowed and she frowned.

"Beneath the cover … are pages, inviolate to the work of water, or of time. Fluttering pages …"

The light around them changed.

There came to the Knight visions – of gold, of wealth, of majesty. There shone lands and realms ready for the asking, the love of the multitude; a world of peace …

Then the water grew more restless, black and rippling with hidden life – and a dark steam seemed to form, pooling across the fragile boundary of air and sea.

And Ava Fitzalan made a low cry – and Cass drew closer in sudden fear.

"Tell me what you see," he commanded.

She pulled away from the well, and her shaking hand rose and covered her eyes.

"I see … my father … *alive again*."

With his heart pounding – and his hand on his weapon – Caspian Hythe waited – for the power, the deadly force of the snare, the *enticement* …

To lessen – for if she falls – if Ava, the strongest of us all can be seduced, what hope is there for those untrained, unprepared, what hope for mere mortals – for anyone else.

But the moment passed – and rich and strong, her voice rang out – in warning.

"There are pages; they turn, passing in and out of their world, the many worlds – and each directs to a different place – a different destiny.

And within each – in the many lands of the Book – there are portals. I saw a place known to me, and to you – in the blackness are many realms, like dark shells, each darker than the last – *and there is She … the One we knew 'Below'.*"

It came to him suddenly, horribly – the memory of his own night with the Queen, as each warred for mastery in a room with a bed – and how

254

he had been so nearly lost, to the power, the seductive call of Power itself …

"Ava – when you were trapped – *'Below'* – who was with you there?"

She turned and regarded him gravely, for she sensed the pith of his question.

"The power you feel now – has always been in me. And in you."

"But I'm not a Fitzalan; not in the line of those that can do what you do."

"No, brother – you're not."

The voice came from out of the shadows – from one of the rough doorways.

And into the dim light of the chamber – Montgomery Quist, with blood across his forehead, and a livid bruise on one cheek stumbled forward – shoved forward by Tam – and last, strode the kin of Percy Onslow.

The eyes of the two young men met.

"I'm not your brother," growled the Mage.

"Aren't you?"

There was no sign of the sword master and Cass' jaw set and his word were harsh.

"Pen. Don't do this."

"Save the lecture, Cass. Do you imagine you're the only one with the rights to power?"

The Knight's words were calm, but implacable.

"He has no rights at all."

255

"What he has – is responsibility. Pen, listen to me. This Thing won't allow you to control it – *once it's open*. I've seen in there – *inside*. No one can stop it, *no one can stop using it* – once it's open. It will eat you. It will devour you – and everything you care for."

The sword master's kin took one step forward; she studied Ava closely.

"What do you know about what I care for. There are those that put limits on what they can – and can't do. I'm not one of them."

The Knight was motionless; blood had dried on the cuts across her face and arms.

Her hair was tousled; sweat had left its tracks on her face. She stood with her boots splattered in mud and gore – as a warrior; muscles firm, relaxed but ready despite her wounds. And Pen could not look away from her, as Ava spoke.

"Just in case you missed it – I'm not one of those, either."

From the Knight's jacket, her wand flashed out, and light curled from its tip.

And the Mage shouted – his dagger was out, but Tam's blade lay close against Monty's throat – and Tam's dagger flew across the chamber straight into Ava's shoulder.

The Knight's wand went skittering off into the dark, as, with a loud cry, the Knight yanked Tam's dagger from her flesh – and dropped it, as if it were blazing hot.

256

Pen leapt forward and seized the weapon from the stone floor – with that terrible and magical blade which had come from Tam – she flew at the Knight.

But the Knight was not unarmed.

Ava drew her own weapon; feinting quickly, she slashed at the girl. The blade sliced through Pen's shirt and laid a bright track of blood on her arm – and with that stroke, at the first drops of spilled blood – a monstrous thing was occurring at the well.

The dark surface of the water over the Book surged into violent life; ripples swirled savagely and a lustrous glow came from the drowned thing.

Then, shuddering – it began to move – rising slowly, as the water above the cloistered chasm slowly began to sink, bringing light and air ever closer to the deadly thing.

The girl fought with all the speed and agility of greater youth – and the ready skills of constant practice. Her bouts with Percy served her well now, as stroke by stroke, she drove the Knight back. In desperation, the Knight whirled in place – and her boot caught Pen full in the face, sending the girl toppling down.

In a fury, Tam cried out – and slammed the hilt of his sword straight across Monty's face – and he threw the helpless man straight at the Knight.

By the far wall, the two crashed down.

A black fume began to curl from the well and the sound of muted howls and voices rose – for Pen had roused and crawled to the very lip of the well.

A flash of gold came from her hand – and the first piece of the Star Taker fell, to float down and land across the Book.

"One down," said Tam.

Then, like a lion with its prey in sight, the son of Abby Fitzalan advanced on the Sorcerer.

Cass stumbled back – the one after the other – the two men circled the deep well with its horrific tenant, as steam curled off the surface of the water – as eerie light marched against darkness, to checker the walls and floors in strange aberrance.

From the side, Monty moaned and Tam spoke again to the Mage.

"I need you alive for just a bit longer."

Then the young Wizard launched himself at Cass.

With his sword glittering like fire, Tam struck again, and again.

Sword against dagger – the wounded one was driven back.

It took all he had for Cass to remain upright, always in defense –and a loud tumult came from the dark doorway – now in deep shadow, Pen had retrieved her weapon and now fought there with all her strength, the sound of blade on blade echoing –

and the girl flew violently backward into the chamber., landing on the stone floor.

And Percy Onslow followed – a sword was in his hand and he hurled the weapon straight at the stunned Mage.

And the Sorcerer rose to his feet with the sword of Iain Fitzalan in his hand and the light glittering off the blade won a round against the rising dark. Again it was blade against blade …

A great cry came from Tam.

He spun, shoved the Mage back, and leapt forward – the last two pieces of the Star Taker in his hand – and Cass was upon him. Locked in a furious struggle, the two men grappled madly – and a second piece of the Taker slid into the water to join its partner on the Book.

Now fire – hot, and glacial and terrible flamed up from the well. It threatened to engulf the two men who still raged at the very lip of the sunken chasm – whose waters yet sank.

And the unholy Book rose slowly – higher and higher.

As with all her might, Pen got to her knees, and hurled the knife given her by an usurper – it struck Cass full in the shoulder.

His cry was lost in a sudden deafening roar of wind as Tam seized the stricken one and, dragging him close to the well's edge, he let fall the third and last piece of the Star Taker.

Down it sank.

Down and close, for each of the three pieces flamed below the shallow waters, and the three convulsed and began to move.

Creeping closer and closer to the others, piece approached piece, until all three touched, and merged into One.

And Tam draped the bleeding arm of the Mage over the edge of the well.

And the Taker blazed with a terrible light, as voices rose avidly from the Book itself – as the blood of the Sorcerer dripped down, into the water – as a bright cloud of blood engulfed the Book, the lock and the chains.

Living water seized the Taker, tipping it away – there came a mighty din of splintering metal – as chains and lock split and sundered – the water sank, and the Book lay bare and brilliant with eager and famished Life.

Yet the chamber was not alone in chaos.

Those living along the coast would remember this day; all would speak of it in times to come – how one day, out of a clear sky, the clouds began to form. How a storm rose from nothing, sending mountainous waves landward, and how lightning slashed across the skies, bolt after bolt, and the heavens burned in wrath.

How from out of the very heart of a *Tempest* – the avid air had come alive – and that life had the Face of a woman, savage and frightful to behold.

For Her wild and streaming hair was lit by lightning, and Her ghastly cry was the voice of the storm itself, of the cyclone that brooks no resistance – that extends no mercy.

And the waves rose like towers, building higher and higher, more and more pitiless, crashing one after another onto the land beside the sea.

As within the cavern – a Book began to open.

And its Pages, curled and writhing, began to slowly turn, imbued with awful life.

The walls of the chamber trembled; still the Thing rose, lusting for the verge of the well – as Tam knelt to the Mage, fallen beside the chasm – and bent to cut the Sorcerer's throat.

Now thundering – the walls of all the caverns shook; the stones and rock of the ceiling close to the height of the pinnacle cascaded down – and blinding sapphire light billowed into the chamber.

Out from the rock itself, from the corridor of stone and sand – the Master strode through the turmoil into the chamber.

Tam seized the bloody hilt of the cursed dagger, yanked it from the Sorcerer's shoulder, and threw it with all his strength – all his hatred – straight at the One – and it struck Him full in the chest.

A thunderclap resounded from high above.

261

The Master pulled the weapon free and the One garbed in human flesh walked to the well where the Book hung in the air – poised.

The Master's hand trembled – but He spoke to the bloody blade; wordlessly, His lips moved – and layer by layer of finely wrought darkness, of black enchantment peeled away until, with its steel shining – pure and clean – the Master held the blade.

And He drew that knife across His bare arm – and held it, dripping, baptised with His own blood – directly over the cursed tome.

Blood spattered down.

With a horrific sound, with the screams of all those lost before and those thirsty for new life – the Book began to close. The golden chains that still hung from the Book sprang to life, binding closely again about the pages and the ancient covers.

And the Book began to sink, as within the well, water foamed and it was fresh and angry with the wrath of storm, with the healing power of the *Tempest* – and the waters rose to reach hungrily for the Book.

The earth awakened – within the well, the walls had begun to split, and the sea rushed in, to cover all, to seal all – as Pen cried out.

The girl raced to the brink of the well – just below her reach lay the Book, sinking quickly and she reached hard – and her fingers stretched out to grasp the unholy thing.

As without warning, thick Blackness reared up from the well, and from the Book – dark, sharp claws took hold of the girl's wrist.

Pen screamed as, stumbling, Percy Onslow raced forward, reaching the girl as the claws pulled her down.

He took hold of her as she went over the verge into the well – and together, they fell, vanishing into the roiling waters whose seething darkness was now red with blood.

In the chamber itself, the walls were threatening to crumble and as they reared and shook – brilliant glowing eyes of russet and green glittered out – then were lost in the dust and brume.

Tam stood alone, watching as Hell opened on earth around him – as all he had sought and worked for vanished before him. Livid with rage, he ran – dimly his form could be seen racing away into the shadows of a dark stone corridor – as the ceiling and walls there collapsed, crashing down behind him, piling high both boulder and sand – choking the way out.

Without, the *Tempest* reached its height – and then the clouds raced away, the gusts of wind dwindled down to breezes – and the waters of the sea fell into calm.

Within – all was silent.

Caspian Hythe coughed and roused completely.

Across the chamber, wrapped in Ava's arms and protected from the chaos – Monty leaned, then pulled himself upright.

And close beside the Sorcerer, lying on the wet sand, beside a well of deep, dark, still water – lay the Master.

In agony, the Mage hauled himself up and crawled to the Master's side.

And Master and Mage regarded one another.

"It's You – it's really You. As alive as I am," whispered the one-time apprentice.

"For the moment. A Brother's blood, you see, …"

The Master winced in pain.

"I had forgotten – how it feels – *life*. *And the rest of it*. See, Mage, it works, it all does work."

And the Sorcerer looked down at the man on the stones, bleeding, and mortally pale.

"Not at this price," he said.

"What price would you give? Caspian, the task is done, the Thing is …"

The Master's voice failed. And His eyes went to the pair across the chamber. Monty was on his knees, weeping, and Ava knelt, silent – as the Master smiled at her.

"Lady."

"My Lord," she whispered.

"See how thy doubts are swept away. And all this by thy hand; he couldn't have done this alone."

264

She stood, nearly blinded with tears.

"As Thy hand was to mine."

"Child, thou hast done *well.*"

The young woman limped forward until she reached Cass' side.

"Stay," she implored.

"I ... *can't.* This shell, not as *resilient* ... But *Caspian* ...

And the Mage's hand covered that of the Master, and the two rings, each to each – began to glow softly as the Master spoke.

"I *am so pleased with thee* –apprentice – Sorcerer – *Wizard* – and more. *Well pleased.* Look for me ..."

And the Master's face grew calm and His voice was low and strong in the silence, with only the soft, sorrowful lull of the sea for reply.

> *Now all My plans are fit and done.*
> *Now all My strength saw battle won.*
> *As Brother countered Brother's strife,*
> *See now the win – and now new life.*
> *Since I have warred with Mine own kind,*
> *Let thine acceptance help Me find*
> *In peace – in rest, a moment's grace,*
> *Before I see once more – thy face.*
> *Spirits and guile – I no longer want.*
> *Now dost thou rise, to guide, enchant.*
> *Temper truth with sophic care, yet*
> *Strive with caution – still beware*

Of snares cast back in times before,
Again shall Evil try the Door.
With coat of many colours, see
The Pentad, ring – my Legacy.
If thou from Darkness safe would be,
'Til I return – keep thou the Key.

Through the storm rent stones above, the sun found its way down.

Light poured onto those below, and the outline of the Master's body wavered in that brilliance.

From above, a fine powder of stone whirled; golden and sparkling it fell, like stardust, over the Mage, and the Knight and the fallen One.

And as the scholar found the strength to join them, that dust grew rich and heavy with moisture, thick with the breath and tears of the sea.

And a rainbow, a light suffused with all colours lit the chamber.

Long it stayed, softening the tears, gilding the face of the Master – releasing and soothing, and burnishing with peace the pageant of triumph – and loss.

CHAPTER 25

KEYS

Caspian Hythe looked down on the keys in his hand.

There on the brass ring that held them captive was the crest of Percy Onslow – and the family motto.

'Quick but careful.'

And so had he been.

Cass laid the keys on the table beside the portfolio that the solicitor had brought. It was sizeable; it would take some time for the Mage to get through it.

But the young man who had opened Percy's home, left the packet of papers – and handed Cass the keys – had assured him there was no need to rush.

Not much older – in actual years – than the Sorcerer, that one had taken a hard look at the cuts and bruises across the Mage's face and arms.

He saw the black silk sling.

Then his eyes had gone to the walls in the hallway, and those of the training studio just across. He'd eyed all the evidence – all the weapons, both modern and archaic.

The Mage had said nothing.

Then the solicitor had shaken his head; he was young, he could not fathom why anyone in the modern age might still do what Percy did.

What Percival Onslow had done – all his life.

Sword master. Lore Master.

Keeper of ciphers – of treasures – of secrets.

A man of power – a spiritual fortress – one whose breadth of life and vision spanned lives and centuries.

A man of family.

The solicitor glanced at his watch, then reminded the Mage – the house and all its contents had been left to him – to one not of Percy's immediate family – except for a handful of items designated for Pen's family – and for Pen herself.

The door closed on the man, peace reigned in the cenotaph where Cass stood, silent and pensive.

Not of the immediate family – how I wish …

The key and the page he had taken from below the tile at the Abbey had gone from his blood-stained pocket to a fine ceramic bowl in Onslow's bedroom.

Even taking the stairs cost him; his arm and shoulder still ached, his body was in strong agreement – a great deal had happened very quickly to this one 'not of the immediate family'. Cass' mind was still in a tumult, still reeling after the events of the last few days.

Was it only days?

It feels like a lifetime; another lifetime.

Whose lifetime, Sorcerer?
Whose?

On the table, in the half- opened packet of legal and personal papers, a single page lay exposed to his view.

'If you are reading this Cass, my dear fellow – it will mean …'

Cass touched the keys close by on the rich wood.

He went to the front door and locked it; it was a treasure that Percy had found, one from the Renaissance – and had fitted for his home. The bolt made a click, heavy and satisfied – as if welcoming the new resident.

Not owner; never that. I am but the guardian of this place – as Onslow was before.

He walked the rooms, so different now that the true owner was gone – and ended in the studio. There across the walls, spread the testament of the man's fidelity – his passion.

His determined courage. What have you taught me, Percy – in the way of the sword – in the way of the Path.

If nothing else – the paramount need, in this 'modern age' for determined courage.

It had been nothing short of a miracle.

For the friend in the coroner's office had been informed, by phone and text – by Percy himself – many days ago – of the likelihood of something going amiss.

269

And had assured him that no foul play would be involved.

No foul play; that phrase covers a lot of ground, both above and below. And none of it plausible or acceptable in the modern sense of the words.

The loss of the niece took some explaining.

Again, the way was made smooth by Percy himself.

Pen's family had been contacted as well by the sword master, just days before that desperate odyssey below the earth – he had proclaimed in the mildest of accents, how tricky and unpredictable the girl's visit had proven – and might continue to be – and how risky life was, especially in the realm of cave exploration.

The sword of Iain Fitzalan was again on the wall of the studio.

Cass had cleaned the blade with a sense of deep pride – and consuming sorrow – and mounted it back in its place. The steel positively glowed; the runes about the blade seemed to have found new life. Now they shown down, expectantly – eagerly – waiting.

Softly, like the afterthought of a dirge, the massive clock in the hall sounded its chimes.

Once more, Cass regarded the weapon – his weapon; he would leave the sword there.

For he planned to remain in the house – his house now, only in the merest sense of the word.

270

And he was waiting, too.

Not far away, in the home loved by Iain Fitzalan – the Knight was making a similar study.

Ava Fitzalan still bore the marks of battle; the cut across her cheek from Pen's dagger would heal – would scar.

It was a record of the Knight's fortitude – to take in hand the task from the Master himself – to take the point in the game, almost from the very moment she had come *'Above'*.

To do the deed.

For not all scars are evil – or even unseemly.

So, she, too, walked through a house now her own, one in which she had taken up the guerdon of stewardship.

Not ownership – for we can never truly own anything from the lives of others.

She ventured into the bay alcove where a sword hung in reverence, in majestic splendour over the entry door. Where a parchment revealing a part of the way had been left – in the faith, the expectation of its discovery – in time.

Now I wonder …

She made her way to the library; silence met her as she pushed open the heavy door. There was the desk where so much had been planned – and accomplished.

There, the books.

Still a wonder – the scope of Fitzalan's collection – since the time a still small girl had come here, eyes wide, with eager mind and insatiable curiosity.

And to whom had come revelation, as the very young woman had taken – in time, in learning, in sensibility – the steps that had led her to a white marble tomb in a cold and misty cemetery.

The books – I'd thought I had been through them all.

Now I wonder – for I see now – I see that I was wrong.

There on the shelf to the side, sequestered between two volumes of a set she had explored dozens of times …

Slender, small – it can only be a journal.

Slowly, for the book was not young – she guided it from its place and held it in her hand.

The room was more than silent now, as if it were watching and listening – and a soft breeze – very alike to that experienced once when an adventurer, a collector and doubting scholar had come to stand in very nearly this same spot.

She looked about the room; all was secure.

Yet, somehow – all is different.

She took the little book, then left, approaching the last door at the end of the hallway.

In her hand she, too, held a key.

Ava stood before the door and admired the fine wood – this was a door very like at least one

272

found in the Onslow home. The ancient grain had been sanded and worked with a precision, a love – that revealed the inner soul of the tree whose life had gone into its creation.

Life – death – beginning – end – creation.

What lies between them, and beneath – is a rabbit hole.

She held up the key – old and lustrous in brass – set it into the lock – and turned the bolt.

She entered into the dark; at her touch, light sprang to life in the lovely globe lamp set upon a desk whose carven glory spread across nearly an entire wall of the small room.

The sleigh bed was made; the cover turned back as if in wait for the occupant' s imminent return.

And the young woman's eyes misted over; there on the edge of the bed was a cloak, one of the few that He had worn.

Ava Fitzalan sat on the bed; taking up the richly woven garment, she brought it to her face. And the scent, like that of sandalwood and myrrh and frankincense – yet as light as memory, came to her.

And she remembered that moment when called and *commanded*, wandering in anguish through the corpse lights of a nether kingdom – she had hearkened – turned, and found the way *back* – and *Up*.

To stand at the Master's side.

What is that?

There on the desk – a small carved box she had not seen before – for not once but several times she had been in this room.

The Knight rose; standing over it, she studied the thing – its perfect proportions, chased in silver, polished and smooth despite its age – and laid in full view.

She opened it.

The light in the room was just enough; it caught, held captive on something that lay within – something golden and bright.

Then the Knight closed the box.

She was already making her phone call as she strode from the room …

As Montgomery Quist closed the last of the massive books piled high before him on his voluminous desk.

So many volumes, for he was a purist and more – he had learned long ago that even resources in the cloud had not yet culled all the learning in the world.

And he disliked the search parameters.

So many books and so thick – so dusty, stacked so high that only the top of his head could be seen had anyone entered this library study.

It was the same room that a young man had visited, when coming to tea – and with the help of a magic word, had brought to life the distant shades of the past – to set into motion everything that had come.

That has come to us all – for I am in the thick of it – these adventures – overflowing with artefacts, with Orbs, attendant Elementals and who knows what other fantastic entities – and let us not forget the beasts.

To say nothing of the Books that eat people.

Like his companions, the man bore evidence of that day; he was bruised, with an elegant band aid across his brow – all sported with a flair that he himself would have designated as flamboyant.

He flipped more pages; they were heavy with age, the parchments long past their prime – and parchment lasted forever as it were – then his bright eyes narrowed.

He never took his eyes from the page before him.

The remaining books; the rest of the piles were gently and very carefully moved aside.

And Montgomery Quist studied that page – of simple parchment – as though he might turn the tables for once and eat the thing himself.

And his lips moved as he followed the words, as his mind took them in – in their significance – in their as yet perfect mystery.

This is it.

What I had been – on a wild hunch – searching for.

And now I am wondering about that wild hunch.

He rose from the desk, looking hard at the book's binding, for it was old, unspeakably old – and he turned away from it.

A little more stiffly, a tad slower than his usual pace – Quist walked away – and looked back, much as he had before.

When the shard lay before me – the piece that Cass had found near the Castle ruins and brought to us all – and I examined right here in this room.

As he was wont to do, in the hope of yet another prospect of irresistible enigma, yet one more blood stirring adventure opening itself before him – he toasted himself.

His snifter was raised to himself – to a safe journey – and safer landing; he did this not once but twice with that same excellent whiskey he had carried in a flask, into what he cheerfully described as 'the underworld'.

With a profound sense of satisfaction, he put down the snifter, and took a deep breath – then, only then – did his bright new phone softly – and he would almost say diabolically – begin to chime.

EPILOGUE

They had all met there – the three, at Abby's bedside.

The lady still slept and they watched over her for awhile, each deep in their own thoughts, each dissecting the meaning, the significance that Abigail Fitzalan had – and that they hoped would continue to have.

Out in the cold air, air that tokened insistently of an early change, a rapid turn of the season, they stood for a moment, looking up at a sky washed by recent storm, with clouds towering and soaring up, stark white domes against the blue.

The ring stayed on the Mage's finger; sunlight caught and held in the small jewel, dazzling to the eyes, sweet to the spirit as the three walked away.

And Montgomery Quist, that old adventurer, raised and swung his treasured cane in the air – and shook it defiantly.

Their passage was not unnoticed.

From the tallest trees beside the place of healing, the thing that Iain Fitzalan had once proclaimed did not exist, rose up, took to the air – its bright gaze was directed downward and its fabulous eyes followed the Professor, the Mage and the Knight for some time.

The creature circled high in the sky.

And its flight took it over a house not far away.

Far below, in the library that Abby loved, where a scholar had witnessed battle and courage to take him to the end of his life, where a young man, a young apprentice learned to put down the cloak of childhood, the chain of anger – and aspire to a cloak of a different source – the presence and passage of the messenger above set a strange wind into life.

Eagerly, carefully did that breeze traverse the rooms, pensively did it linger in the library. Papers rustled across the floor where a fate had been decided – and seen by none, the Sylph took form from the living air.

Sad and beautiful were the Elemental's eyes, glowing brightly as that Being of air, of spirit hovered over the desk – where His gentle, forceful breath sent the tarot cards of Abigail Fitzalan up – to flutter down upon the floor.

With His mane of light ridden hair floating, the Sylph regarded the cards; there was the card for Death – for transformation, and there the one signifying the rise of the unknown one, who had come to battle – and there in the centre – the Page of Wands.

Floating into the air itself, the Sylph vanished.

The cards came to complete rest; and as the form of the Gryphon soaring high above, left this place, on the desk, the Orb, the Eye of the First – roused into strange and eerie life.

Glowing now in the room, figures and objects took to motion in the heart of the deadly globe – and when the winged One had left all far behind – only then did the Orb sink back into restless sleep.

When the figures of the three humans had dwindled to little more than specks – even to the Gryphon's vision, it flew higher, its broad wings caressed by the icy clouds as it sped away.

Its course took it high above the towns and cities that we know as real – that we lean upon as trusted foundations in this, our unpredictable, fickle world.

The Gryphon traveled south and west until it spied a strange needle, a pinnacle of stone reaching up past thick green trees and shrubs – and the creature descended, until it perched on the still surviving lip of the broken roof of the ruined 'Isle'.

The Gryphon cast a bright gaze downward, seeking out the world below the torn stones.

Rock clattered down as those massive talons moved over the surface of the roof.

Stones plummeted down into a pool, vast and green, where dark water, risen again to its proper level churned and surged in dim copy of the true sea's tides.

The sound of water echoed in the chamber where lay the miniature ocean.

But the calm of the field after battle is not one of peace.

It is the calm of remorse, of death – of new beginning.

The copper feathers across the head and body of the Gryphon fluttered; it flicked its wings and the long claws shifted – and from the great creature's savage beak came a low warble.

There was movement far below in the near drowned crypt.

And the Gryphon's eyes –green and gold and russet – glowed as it eagerly watched what now transpired on the stony path beside the captive ocean's basin, for that lesser cousin of the greater had grown silent and still.

Still and quiet, like a true crypt or the sepulcher that holds the memory of an occupant and not an actual form, was the cavern – waiting.

Now from the scattered patchwork of light and dark that the sun cast in defiance, brightening the floor of the cavern – darkness swirled.

Swirling, taking its substance from the sodden rocks themselves, from darkness came the form of smokeless fire, and out from the living stone, the Djinn – Ariel strode.

The Djinn stood slight and silent beside this fertile footnote of the sea's might and Ariel breathed deep the brine-sweet scent of the sea.

Free – yet not free.

Fire flickered about the tall, earthly form of the Djinn; fire glittered in the eyes of the sprite – as ripples began to swim again across the dark waters at his feet.

Labouring, heavy and agitated, they grew – as the Fate turned once again – and the present kindled into new life.

With His eyes blazing with passion Ariel looked down, to what lay on the stones beside the well – glistening and expectant.

There, nearly obscured by the dark – was the pile of books, hoary and ancient.

There, in pieces, yet enduring and imperishable in any world – lay the staff of the Other – and beside it – a cloak.

It was that same cloak that had drawn from both darkness and light – to weave that rough magic, that a young man had witnessed long, long ago, and forged into golden verse.

Radiant was the smile that lit the dark face of the Djinn, and Ariel stepped back.

The water trembled, swirls of light made cautious way across the rippling darkness.

As from beneath the surface of the water, fingers crossed that boundary of dark, and a hand reached up, to find its way into the air.

It rose, higher and higher – and now the arm followed, white, and pale and trembling, freeing itself from the deep, from the clinging waves of the past.

Weakly at first, then strong and hale – the arm reached, the long fingers stretched, searching earnestly – determinedly, until they touched the prize.

Then they closed, to knot themselves tightly and powerfully in the dazzling fabric of the Wizard's Cloak.

END OF BOOK THREE